PR Publications LLC

P.O. Box 32985

Detroit, MI 48232

pr_publications@hotmail.com

First PR Publications LLC trade paperback edition 2012, for information about special discounts for bulk purchases, please contact PR Publications special sales, Attn: Mr. Paul Tate at (313) 932-0710 or by email at pr_publications@hotmail.com.

Manufactured in the United States of American, ISBN# 978-0-615-60852-5. Copyright © 2010 by Rio. Cover design by Ms. Regina Barnes and photography by Mr. Lester Sloan.

Coming of Age

By

Rio

Acknowledgments

It's been a long journey but we here, I guess it's true that if you invest energy into something positive, things will eventually fall in place. First I wanna thank the Higher Power for giving me the strength and perseverance to put the pen to the paper and make this happen. To the most important women in my life, my Grandmother, Mother and Shawnie. I LOVE YALL SO MUCH!! Without yall this is not possible. Thanks for putting up with me, all the researching, ripping and running, and just having patience with me period. Thanks for showing me the true meaning of family and loyalty. To the rest of my immediate FAM, Jake, Tee, Big Fin, Tina, Taylor, T'asia, Tierra, and Ashley. Everybody in that house on Pulford. Bubs what's the deal homie? Yall my everything, our unit is small, but the love is large. To my Pops, we came a long way, the more I get to know you, the more I get to know myself, your support motivates me, love you. (Worth more than platinum) My Granddad, your wisdom is priceless, thanks for your continuing support and working your magic on the cover. Lorraine, how are you, thanks for showing me love out of that big heart of yours. My Aunt Aisha, everyday is a learning process with us. Thanks for your insight, getting to know you is an adventure, I never want to end. To the rest of my family, were not as close as I'd like, but I never stop thinking of yall.

To my brothers from another, Matt, Tre, Ro, nothing lasts forever, it's only a matter of time before we reunited, winning again. It's only three words that can describe our bond, "you already know." (smile) PT, what can I say? Thanks for believing in me. You one of the last real ones left, they don't make them like us no more. PR Publications let's get it, same rules, different game. To the whole hood Black Bottom / Macktown / M&M stand up!!! Everybody from Benson to Canton, etc. Kev whatup doe? Remember them late nights in the spot? I'm still grinding, different platform though. My Westside fam over there off Elmhurst, R.I.P. Tremaine. I miss you so much my nigga, we made history. I know you looking down on me proud, I'm working my nigga. Damian, damn, I wish I could bring you back, but I to stick to the script and follow the plan. Nell, Crill, CT, Rio, Bill whatup!!! To all the oldheads from the East to the West who took the time out to pull me to the side and sprinkle me.

Yall did a good job raising me. It's too many of yall to name, but yall know who yall are. Thanks to yall, I've always been wise beyond my years. All that game I soaked up on Meldrum paid off. I love yall. To all the soldiers we lost either indirectly or to this game that we play, yall gone, but not forgotten, rest in peace.

Peaches, all those books you use to send me paid off huh. Don't know where we went wrong, but it's always love here. Loyalty is my weakness. To my Little Secret, thanks for your never-ending support. You are a rare jewel, real talk. To Chemore, thanks for helping a stranger. Q a.k.a Courtney Coles, my artist, good looking out for the logo. Regina Barnes, my cover artist, you did your thing girl. Malloy Incorporated, my printer / editor thanks for working with me, I know I'm a piece of work. (smile)

To all my fellow soldiers on lock. "Do-Dirt, Jabo, T-Rod, Lil Rudy, Rich, Rumar, Freak, Ray, AV, ATL, Chino, Kwam, Bern, Haskell, Gus, AZ, Roc, Los, Brizz, Man-Man, Joe, Maine, BK, Brightmoor, Shock, 'Y', LK, BO, Slick, Spank you free now, but whatsup with

you? George my counsel we gone make it!!! DJ
whatsup!!! Hold ya head up there. And all the other
thoroughbreds I crossed paths with behind these walls.
Shout out to you if you followed the rules and stuck to
the script. Hold your head, its light at the end of the
tunnel, don't give up before you get there. Everybody
who read this book back in 2010 when it was just a
manuscript, thanks for the feedback.

Slime Poe!!!! The realest dude in the Nasty Nati.
Everybody on Facebook, thanks for the love, it keeps me
pushing. Wayne from Southwest whatup! Detroit the
City that raised me. They say I rep too hard, I say it
ain't no such thing. To all my out-of-state peoples, yall
know who yall are, hold it down. JD whatup doe!
Thanks for holding ya boy down when it counted the
most. J-Smooth what's understood don't need to be
said. Keep doing you and stay on your job homie. To
everybody out there who held me down and showed me
love during this bid, whether it was for 2 weeks or 2
years, you are appreciated. Anybody I forgot, charge it
to my mind, not my heart. Last but not least thanks to
all the authors who paved the way. Special thanks to all
the readers, stick with me, I won't let yall down.

Much Love,

Remy

For questions or comments on book, visit the author at prpublications.org or on Facebook (Jeremy Mulligan)

R.I.P. Damian and Tremaine, my brothers from another.

For all those who started hustling with a goal in mind, but somewhere along the way became addicted to the allure of the streets.

Prologue

Rome

I remember it like it was yesterday. It had to be around '95', '96', I was 13 going on 25. I mean I wasn't a bad seed or nothing, in and out of juvenile or nothing like that. I did a lot of observing and took in a lot at an early age. This particular day it was the summer time , late summer to be exact. I was on my usual mission to my room to just chill and get my mind right. I always been anti-social, but when you exposed to a lot, and game is being thrown your way from all angles, every now and then you need time to yourself to reflect and just soak it all up. I walk in my room and it's a white VHS tape sitting on top of my VCR. How it got there or who put it there, I still don't know to this day. Curiosity led me to pop it in A.S.AP. A couple of my uncles and oldheads from the hood had just got back from Miami and they brought back some live footage. They brought all the cars out, everything they was driving was exotic. Not just your average foreign whips, these boys had them big boy toys out. Flying down the strip of South Beach in the Porsche Carrera, the Lambo, the CLK's, the BMW 7 series, the list goes on. It was like a scene from one of your favorite videos today.

Money wasn't an issue, the only issue was arguing over how it was gonna get spent first. They were rubbing shoulders with the latest rappers and entertainers but that didn't shock me, what shocked me was how they were outshining them. It was like the roles were reversed, the celebrities were the groupies. On the tip like, "I wonder who theses dudes are?" Honestly, it felt good to know that these were dudes I was around everyday. I got a rush, and a sense of pride overwhelmed me. These were my people, my oldheads, the same ones who were trying to keep me away from the game, but at the same time pulling me back in. If I had any doubts they were erased at that moment. I knew what I wanted to do right then and there, I knew I wanted a taste. Like everything else I witnessed, that tape had a major effect on me. Product of my environment I guess you can call it. Often people on the outside looking in like to call that a misconception. Yeah it's a fact that every person from the hood is not a thug or criminal. The ghetto has produced doctors, lawyers, even judges. When it's all said and done though, those weren't the people I saw everyday. I don't know any of them personally. When they make it, do they come back? Where do they go? The older females I had a crush on weren't praising them. They didn't own four or five cars, or never wore the same thing twice. What seem shallow to you, may mean the world to me.

Jay-Z said it best, "Everything I seen made me everything I am." If only at that time I knew the other side of the fence though. The addiction I would later succumb to, stronger than any drug known to man. Born in it not sworn in it, yeah I like that. I didn't choose this life, it chose me, or did I? This is our story, well part of it, I'll let you be the judge.

Chapter 1

1992

"Boy you better get in there and watch that damn wrestling, after I done spent my money on that shit."

"Alright Ma, I'm just getting some Kool-Aid dang." Rome said with attitude. It was pay-per-view night, but not pay-per-view as in the heavyweight title. No tonight was the night that the Ultimate Warrior could challenge Hulk Hogan for his title belt. Once Little Rome got his necessities, he was glued to the TV screen. Born Jerome Wilson, everybody called him Rome for short. At the age of 9, Rome was a big WWF fan. If you told him it was fake and most of the wrestling consisted of acting, he'd argue you to death. Debra loved her son, he was her pride and joy. She loved her three year old daughter the same, but Rome was her first born or like she used to say, the child she planned to have.

She sat at the kitchen table drinking her signature drink. A double shot of Seagram's Gin and a glass of beer. From the outside looking in people probably looked at her as an unfit parent. In Jerome's eyes she was as good as it gets. So what she had a crack habit or wasn't the best dresser or didn't own a car. She was there for him and made things happen. Tonight was a prime example. It could be worse, growing up in the hood that was more than you can say for a lot of people.

(Wrestling commentator)

"The Ultimate Warrior slams Hulk Hogan, he's down, Ultimate Warrior climbs the ropes." "Hogan is down, Hogan is down!"

"What the fuck!!" Debra could be heard screaming from the kitchen. Three policeman burst through the door with guns drawn. Rome was so into the match, he didn't notice the officer with his gun drawn aimed at his head. Rome didn't bulge or shed a tear, great poise for a nine year old. Couldn't say the same for Debra though, she was hysterical.

"Get that fucking gun away from my baby!"

"Where is Donte Jackson?" The officer asked not once lowering his gun.

"I don't know who the hell that is!" Debra screamed.

"Don't fucking lie to me, we know this is his Auntie house; He ran this way."

Awakened from her sleep, Rome's grandmother Ms. Patti walked down the steps calmly approaching the officers, but inside she was steaming.

"First yall need to put those guns down, don't yall see children in here?" Ms. Patti talked to the officers as if they were kids. "Donte don't live here, he ain't been here, so yall can get the hell out of my house. You don't have a warrant and I know the law better than you think."

"Sorry ma'am, we didn't mean any disrespect we gone be on our way." It was too late for apologies, the damage was already done.

"And yall gone have to pay for my door!" Ms. Patti yelled as the cops were exiting.

"Sure ma'am you'll hear from us," said one of the cops while he was entering the patrol car, but those were false promises. Ms. Patti would never hear from them and she knew it. This was an everyday thing in the hood. One of the reasons why the people had no faith in law enforcement, they'd rather take matters in their own hands and deal with the consequences.

Ms. Patti sat on the couch rubbing Rome's head, "You alright baby?"

"Yeah I'm cool grandma," Rome answered without looking up. All he was concerned with was the wrestling on TV still.

"What the hell Donte done did now?" Debra said.

"I don't know, ain't no telling with his ass. This the first place they come looking for somebody." Ms. Patti responded with a frown on her face.

See, even though she only had one son, one daughter, and five grandkids, Ms. Patti was like the hood Auntie, mother or whatever you wanna call it. She was always there for somebody whether she condoned it or not. Illegal or legal, she was loyal and rode for the cause. Definitely one of a kind, who knows how it got this way, she was a lovely church going woman who always wanted the best for her kids, but the hood had

14

other plans. I mean don't get me wrong, she was a retired schoolteacher with no felonies, but even she got caught up in some mess along the way. Which is why she wore an ankle monitor and couldn't leave the house for thirty days.

Debra was her oldest and only daughter. Her future looked promising at first, she attended one of the best private schools on Detroit's eastside. She stayed under the radar and didn't let the hood get the best of her. She went off to college back east at Providence and had Rome. About three years later all hell broke loose. Freebasing was the thing back then, and you know what they say, curiosity killed the cat. Hanging with them white girls on campus, it seemed like the thing to do. Ever since then it's been downhill, she ended up being expelled from school, came back and crack had took over like everywhere else. She been in and out of rehab numerous times, she'd be clean for a minute, but it never stuck. It's hard to shake a habit when your environment don't change. Everyone who knew her before, hated to see her go out like that, but they loved her just the same. Even though she was smoking, she was still one hellava hustler.

Shane was her younger brother by seven years. If three words could sum him up, it would be "fly ass nigga." Shane had a closet full of everything from big block Mauri gators, Gucci, Coogi, Polo, whatever was in at the time. If it cost money and looked decent, he had it on. He kept some type of hustle, but wasn't ten toes in it. All of his boys were heavy in the game though, Shane was a laid back smart cat.

Then you got Trece, Tone, and Donte, Uncle Frank's three kids who was Ms. Patti's brother. They all were around the same ages so all their friends and mostly everybody else in the hood was always around and considered family. So you could see how Ms. Patti got the label as the hood grandmother. Which is one of the reasons why the police had just kicked the door in. Rome's home was the hangout for all the doughboys, fiends, and players around the neighborhood. A group of dudes would always be in front of the house all day drinking with the music banging. Any given day you might see someone get they ass beat, shot at or arrested. Not to mention the drug sales that went on, on the daily basis in or in front of the house. At times Rome hated it, at times he loved it. It was a double edged sword, I mean sometimes it was embarrassing, but as he got older, he started to look at the advantages.

You had the game right in front of you. You had dudes like Geno, Ski, and Big Dre pulling up in all that foreign shit. Any given day, it'll be a 600, 745, or Lex Coupe out front, Acura's the list goes on. It was a downside depending on how you looked at it. This was the eastside of Detroit mid 90's Mack & Mt. Elliot, also known as Black Bottom or Macktown. This was the slums for real, no bullshit. Where the grass don't grow, murders go unsolved. It looked like a ghost town, everybody walking around strung out. Every man for himself, didnt nobody wanna see anybody else come up. Fiends roaming everywhere, two and three drug houses on each block. Some people were scared to visit if they didn't know anybody.

It may sound exaggerated but if you from the hood, then you can relate. Rome's house wasn't an exception. He was always embarrassed to have friends over, except for immediate ones. Let's see, you had Rome, Shane, Ms. Patti, Debra, Trece, Carrie (Rome's

16

little sister), Dominique, and Trina (Trece's daughters) all living there. Eight people under one roof, one bathroom and one breadwinner made it hectic at times. Like having to run across the street to fill up pots of water, bring it back and put it on the stove, until it got hot enough to take a bath in. Hiding your school money every night so your Mom and Aunt wouldn't steal it in the middle of the night to try and go cop with. Rome even remembers one morning while he was getting ready for school, watching his mother try to steal a sack of rocks out of his cousin's pocket while he slept. All types of stuff went on in the house, but with the bad comes the good. Like staying up late watching Scarface with his cousin Tone or seeing Shane bring home some of the baddest chicks he ever seen. At nine years old Rome saw a lot and knew a lot, more than people gave him credit for. You know how the saying goes, kids are smarter than you think.

Chapter 2

1995

Knock! Knock! (Knocking on the door)

"Who is it?" Debra asks.

"Donnie!"

"Who?"

"Donnie!"

"Alright hold on, how my baby doing?" Debra said while opening the door.

"I'm alright, is Rome here?"

"Yeah he upstairs with that music blasting, his ass gone go deaf."

("Nigga I'm straight ballin! I got a half ounce I wish it was a keylo.") Tupac's Thug Life album could be heard coming through the speakers. Donnie burst through the door while Rome was rapping with Pac.

"Don what up though?"

"You ain't Pac nigga," Don said laughing.

Donnie grew up like three blocks away, he was brought up in the same environment, pretty boy, light-skinned with hazel eyes, he lived with his mom, his father got killed when he was seven years old. Him and Rome were best friends since preschool and at the age of 13, they were inseparable.

"I'm glad you came through, I was about to go to the store for moms," Rome told Don. Debra caught them while they were walking out the door. "Here boy, bring me a double shot of Seagram's too." On the way to the store, Rome was approached by plenty of dopefiends and crackheads. They all loved Rome and was friendly with them. They knew he was Debra's baby and that made him popular with them.

"Hey Rome."

"Hey Sunshine."

"Where your mom at?" Sunshine the youngest trick on Mack Ave. asked.

"She at the house," Rome said with his face frowned.

"Oh ok, tell her I'll see her in a minute then."

"Rome my man what's happening?" "What's happening Bobby Joe?" Bobby Joe was what we called the Arabs that worked at the corner store. In the 'D', mostly Arabs owned the liquor stores, gas stations, and coney island restaurants. You could find a liquor store or coney island on almost every corner in the hood. Some of the Arabs were in the streets heavy. The same liquor store you bought liquor from, you could buy anything from heavy weight to food stamps. Bobby Joe and them had the police from the local precinct on they side, so it wasn't no big deal to them. They did what they wanted, they were even one of the only stores who sold liquor on Christmas Day, they just doubled the price of every bottle.

19

"Hey you want something from the coney island?" Rome asked Don.

"Nah, I'm cool, I just ate."

"Damn!!" Rome shouted. "Look at Donte over there fucking ol boy up. He gone kill that nigga." Donte picked up a half of concrete block that was cracked from the pavement and dropped it on dude head. Rome and Don watched in awe from the coney island parking lot.

"Man, I think that's Ike from off Charlevoix St."

"Hell yeah that is that nigga," Don responded. Donte's boy Fonz and some of the other fellas pulled up and was trying to get Donte off of him. Donte had his gun drawn and his adrenaline rushing, a bad combination. That's how you catch a body on some stupid shit. Donte wasn't trying to hear it though, he snatches Ike's chain off his neck and throws it in the sewer. "Bitch as nigga you don't put nothing else on your neck until you have my money," he screams aggravated.

"Man that nigga could of gave that chain to me," Don said laughing. Meanwhile Don and Rome make their way back to Rome's house. Rome drops his mother stuff off and they proceed to Don's house.

"Hey Don you wanna go over Dana house?"

"I don't know you think her grandma home?" Don said answering a question with a question.

"Shit who cares?"

"Whatever nigga don't act tough now, you wasn't saying that last time she was home." Don wasn't even in the house good before he threw Tupac on. (music playing) ["first off fuck your bitch and the click you claim, Westside when we ride come equipped with game, "you claim to be a player, but I fucked your wife, we bust on Bad Boy leave them slumped for life."] Don and Rome sang along with Pac. Around this time '94, '95 you couldn't tell Pac nothing, you couldn't tell Rome and Don nothing either.

"Hey Rome, hold on I wanna show you something." Donnie came back with a raggedy six shot 2-5.

"Where you get that shit from?" Rome asked with his eye-bows raised.

"I hit a lick on my brother for it, he don't use it anyway."

"Man it only got two bullets in it," Rome finds it funny. What you gone do with this?"

"Chill dog, I'm a get some more, crackhead Dave gone get me some."

"Whatever dog, let's be out."

"That's whatsup, Jake called me earlier so we can go see whatsup with him," Don said in unison. Jake was the third musketeer, he was they other half. Jake was a problem child, always into something. Live wire whatever you wanna call it. His mom ran the streets 24/7. She was the type who had a different boyfriend every other week. She dressed nice and all Jake's friends were in love with her. She was a good mother when she was around, but that was seldom. Don and Rome proceeded to walk to Jake's house. Once they reached his home, after banging on his door for about ten minutes, they were ready to leave.

"Man he probably up there sleep," Rome said irritated. "Oh naw here he come now. What up doe? Damn dog what you up there doing?"

"Nothing man fixing me something to eat. What's going on, what yall got up?"

"Shit we was gone stop over Dana's house." Rome responded.

"Man ever since she gave yall, yall first piece of pussy yall been all over that broad. She not thinking bout yall, yall niggas is whipped." Jake was on a roll, he knew how to get them wild up.

"Man that's that nigga," Don spoke up, looking towards Rome.

"Shut-up you the one that brought up going over there," said Rome in defense.

"Man whatever, holdup let me smash this food right quick." Jake interrupted.

"Dog that's all you eat is Ramen noodles." Don said like he didn't know the drill.

"That's only cause that's the only thing in here. Hey Rome, Don showed you that little B-B gun he got?"

"This ain't no B-B gun nigga, you tripping."

"Might as well be with just them two bullets in it." (laughing) "Yeah keep laughing it'll be ready in a minute." Don said in defense. The three made their way out and before the door hardly closed, Don fired up a blunt. Instantly he almost coughed his lungs up. Jake was anxious, "Damn where you get that from Concord?"

Naw, I got it off Heidi, here you go said Don while handing the blunt to Jake. "Hold that down, there go Ski," Rome shouted. Ski flew down the block in his S600 tapping the horn twice acknowledging them. Man that thing look better and better everytime I see it, I gotta get me one of them." "Man shutup and pass them greens," Jake didn't wanna hear it, he was trying to get high. After five long puffs he tried to pass it to Rome. "Here you go dog."

"Naw, I'm cool yall go head."

"You still scared of the weed nigga?" Jake asked.

"Dog ain't nobody scared, I'm just cool."

"Scared Ms. Patti gone beat that ass," Don threw is two cents in. All three of them burst out laughing. Meanwhile, they were a few houses down from Dana's house. Jake spotted her as they sped up the pace.

"Whatsup ugly?" Dana said, she was joking but had the serious face on.

"Shut the fuck up," Jake said with authority knowing the comment was directed at him. Dana was older than the boys by 1 ½ years. She was 15 going on 25. If you didn't know any better you'd think she was at least 20. She wore all her clothes like they were painted

23

on and she had a grown woman body. She was the average hoodrat, but she thought she was the shit cause older cats outside the hood stayed hollering at her.

That's how it was in Black Bottom, a female head would get swole for the simple fact that a dude from another hood wanted to get with her. The hood could be just as grimy, it didn't matter. She gave Rome and Don some pussy six months ago, out of spite just to be there first and mess with their head. She didn't let them do anything since, she'd tease the hell out of them but nothing would happen.

"What yall little nappy headed fools want? Yall need to be somewhere trying to get some money, cause them forces is busted," Dana was cracking herself up.

"Oh don't worry, we got a money getter right here," Don said while lifting the 2-5 in the air.

"Boy you don't even know what to do with that."

"Yeah, but I know what to do with that though," said Don smiling and licking his lips.

"No you don't, that's why you ain't got none since then." Oohh! Oohh! The boys were laughing and instigating. "Rome, I don't know what you laughing at, with that little thing you working with." Dana said giggling.

"You wasn't saying that six months ago." Rome said in defense.

"And Jake you ain't had no pussy since it had you."

"Shut-up bitch," Jake said with the serious face. Rome interrupted before it turned into something else. "Naw but for real Dana, when you gone stop playing?"

"She not thinking bout yall, Odell from 7 Mile be blowing her back out, I be seeing his Pathfinder spin the block. Shit that nigga bout thirty ain't he?" Jake was trying to hit a nerve.

"So what and? Anyway mind your own damn business."

"Damn so it's like that?"

"Like what Rome?"

"What we not old enough for you now?"

"Yeah what you like child molesters?" Dana was feeling cornered.

"Shit, yall boys need to get yall cash up. For real though cause, (Dana singing) [Ain't nothing going on but the rent, you gotta have a J-O-B, if you wanna be with me."]

Jake cut her off, "shut your ass up, you don't even got no rent."

"I know, but that's my shit, my Auntie always playing that when I come over. Anyway my Grandma about to pull up in a minute so yall gotta get to stepping." Dana was moving too fast, so were the boys, but when you the one doing the moving you never can realize it until it's too late.

25

"Man, we gotta put something together A.S.A.P." Don said walking with his head down. Looking at his shoes reminded him how bad he needed some dough in his pocket.

"Yeah I fell you," said Rome.

"Hey put Rome up on what we was talking about." Jake said talking to Don.

"Oh yeah you know they got one of them Rave parties coming to the hood this weekend. We can catch some of them white boys coming out of there and hit them. You know they be having a couple dollars on them."

"What you gone use, that bullshit you got?" Those were the first thoughts that crossed Rome's mind.

"Yeah why not?"

"Man you tripping."

"Dog them white boys gone give whatever they got up, Don responded. They already be extra scary cause they be in the hood, they not use to this shit down here. We probably can come up with two or three g's easy. They be having a lot of money on them cause soon as they get in the party, they be ready to cop. The rec let my Uncle Drew work security that one time and he always talking bout that shit."

Jake interrupted, "plus they be having all types of links and watches on, so drunk and high they already be off balance not knowing what's going on." At 14 years old these boys made it sound good like they had it all figured out. Rome was open, they had him sold.

"Yeah you right, we can put it together, I'm bout to get up out of here though."

The boys make their way home in separate directions. Rome couldn't wait to make it home his stomach was growling. He was moving faster than a fiend who just copped some stones. As he was walking down Mack Ave. he spoke to all the prostitutes and crackhead pimps he'd known all his life. Approaching his house, it was the same old thing.

It looked like a miniature block party in front of the house. Everyone was there today, Big Dre, Ski, Shane, Donte, Tone, Monty B, Ronnie Moe, Bebe from the Westside, Big Troub, Little Cool and Larry D. Rome breezed by spoke to a couple people and went in the house.

"Hey grandma?"

"Hey baby, how's it going?"

"Where my momma at?"

"I don't know I think she went to the store."

"What yall cook?"

"She made some hamburger helper and french fries. She on her way back with the hamburger buns." Rome was ready to eat without the buns, he was hungrier than a hostage. Debra always took thirty minutes to go to the store when it was only a two minute walk. That's because she really used this time to score, going to the store was just a pump fake. Rome loved his mother to death and wouldn't trade her for the world. Despite his surroundings and harsh circumstances he had

27

a good upbringing. They made something out of nothing and took care of him and his sister the best they could, but sometimes the best just wasn't good enough. Ms. Patti pretty much held the whole family down. Shane and some of the other fellas made sure Rome stayed fresh and kept the latest kicks on his feet. They all had love for him and wanted something better for him. Call it hypocritical but they wanted to see him make it. Rome just saw what he wanted to see though. Plus as you get older your feet get bigger and them shoes get more expensive, so do your fashion appetite. Sooner or later you gotta get your own.

Chapter 3

The Jeffries Projects was located towards downtown Detroit not too far from the Chrysler freeway, better known as I-75. Heroin was big in Detroit, always been big since the 60's, it's part of Detroit culture. If you don't know read some Donald Goines. You could get a bag for as low as three dollars. The Jeffries Projects was a dopefiends rest haven. You couldn't sell that cut up bullshit around here, this is where the connoisseurs were. In the eighties you could find people coming from outside the state just to cop from the Jeffries. It wasn't like it used to be but in 97 it was still a goldmine. This is where Donte made his money. See yall call it heroin, raw or dope. In the 'D' we call it dog food, and Donte had that good dog. His heroin was taking a 7, which mean you could cut it seven times and it still would be potent. Donte was a true hustler though, and one of his philosophies was quality before quantity. So he only cut his dope two times and his clientele was crazy. The nigga didn't even have no set hours, he put it down whenever and they would come running. That's what good dog did for you, it basically sold itself. It was nothing for him to make six or seven grand in a couple of hours, all off hand to hand.

Donte was 25 years old, he'd been getting money for awhile but he wasn't considered big boy status. He wasn't the flashy type, so if you didn't know any better, you'd think he was barely making it. The Jeffries was home to his babymother of four Meka. She was from Black Bottom, but she had family in the Jeffries. Eventually she moved to the projects for the same reason everybody else did, the forty dollar a month rent. Today was there oldest son Jamal eighth birthday, and they were having a little B-day bash for him. Meka

29

walked outside while Donte was flipping burgers on the grill.

"Damn Donte you gone drink the whole half gallon of Hennessey to yourself?" she asked.

"Shut the fuck up, I could drink three of these, if I wanted to."

"I know you need to slow your ass down."

"Man leave me alone and do something useful with yourself. Go in there and stop Tanisha from crying and do something with Monica hair. Damn!! I shouldn't have to tell you shit like that."

Meka didn't really mind when he talked to her like that alone, but she despised it in front of company. A couple of the fellas were over just chilling and getting they sip on. Fonz, Ronnie Moe, and Meka's younger brother Stoney. Meka loved Donte but she always felt like she could do better. Eventhough she had four kids, her body was still intact. She had some nice B-cup breasts with an ass like Trina. She kind of resembled Malinda Williams, you know the chick that played in the movie "The Wood" the younger version of the chick Omar Epps character was in love with. Meka did her little thing on the side, but nothing too serious. Despite the fact they had kids together, she had a soft spot for Donte. Plus she was a hoodrat and he was a hood nigga so she felt they belonged together.

In her mind, the physical abuse and heavy drinking she dealt with was all part of the program. Hours later, Donte stumbles into the house to find Meka in her room laying on her stomach.

"Girl get your ass up," Donte said while slapping her on the ass.

"Boy you play too damn much, I'm trying to get some sleep before I put the kids to bed. Fonz and them still outside?"

"Yeah."

"Man they need to take they ass home for a change," Meka said aggravated.

"Girl be quiet and come here," Donte said while massaging her ass.

"Stop..." Meka said not really wanting him to stop. Donte begin kissing her neck and fondling her breast, while Meka is rubbing his dick. Donte takes her half dollar size nipples into his mouth while rubbing her clit with his thumb and index finger. Becoming hot and bothered, Meka couldn't take it anymore. She jumps up and snatches Donte's pants down and pulls his dick out of his boxers and goes to work sucking and stroking. Her head game was phenomenal. Reason being she was one of them females whose pussy got wet at the thought of giving head let alone doing it. Donte couldn't take it anymore, he spreads her ass cheeks and slides in from behind. To this day he was amazed at how tight she remained after having four kids.

"Oohh!!....Fuck me daddy! Ohh.., fuck me hard, oh I love this dick," Meka screamed as Donte pounds away like it's no tomorrow. Meka was throwing it back like Mitchell & Ness. Every two or three strokes, she would rotate her ass in a circular motion. She knew what she was doing and it was working.

"Arrgh! Arrgh! Here I come baby," Donte moaned.

"Uh huh yes baby come for me." Donte was pounding away giving his all. Meka turned around and took all of Donte into her mouth. She sucked and jerked until he came and swallowed every bit of it.

"Oh shit damn baby," Donte laid back breathing heavily. "You still know how to put it on a nigga."

"Enjoy it motherfucker, this might be the last you see of this," Meka snapped.

"What the fuck is you talking bout?" Donte was shell-shocked.

"Nigga I heard about your little escapade with them little dirty bitches Shondra and them from the King Homes."

"Man get the fuck out of here, you'll believe anything."

"Nigga shutup cause Stoney fuck with the bitch sister."

"So what that mean?"

"Donte don't play stupid!" she snapped. "What you think I don't got niggas," Meka said while running up in Donte's face.

"Bitch calm your ass down," Donte shouted as he slapped Meka across the face. Meka fell to the ground and as she was trying to get up, he kicked her in the stomach and punched her in the face.

He was taking it too far as usual. "Ahh!! Ahh!!" Meka could be heard screaming all the way outside. Stoney was in the bathroom when he heard his sister screaming. Donte was his homie but Meka was his sister. He didn't let it show, but he was getting fed up with Donte using his sister as a punching bag. That along mixed with the jealously of him was a bad combination. Stoney was at the point of no return and it made it worse that his nieces and nephews were witnessing it. Fonz and Ronnie Moe were outside drinking, talking to some project chicks from the building behind them. Meanwhile Stoney in his own boiling rage grabs his 12 gauge from under the couch cushion and runs towards the room. The door kicks in snapping Donte out of his zone momentarily.

"Nigga get your muthafuckin hands off my sister!" Stoney cocks the shotgun for emphasis.

"What the fuck you cocking that for like you gone shoot something? You the reason this shit started, running your mouth about them dusty ass bitches." Donte said like he wasn't fazed.

"Nigga fuck you," Stoney shouts still aiming the gauge at Donte's chest.

"Put the gun down," Meka said screaming and crying. Her face was looking like Martin Lawrence after he fought Tommy Hearns on his sitcom. "Put it down Stoney, it's alright." By this time they had gained the attention of Jamal, who was standing right behind Stoney unbeknownst to him.

"That's right listen to big sis, nigga you ain't gone kill nothing, I basically raised you." Donte was

33

looking Stoney directly in the eyes as he was talking while at the same time he had a smirk on his face, trying to intimidate him. Either he thought this was a joke or he actually thought Stoney was scared. "Put the fucking gun down bitch ass...., Boom!! Boom!! Arrgh! Arrgh! (screaming) Stoney shot Donte twice in the chest before he could get his words out.

"Nooo! No! Boy what you done did," Meka screams as she leans over Donte's body. Little Jamal was horrified as he watched his uncle shoot his father. Sad to say, his birthdays would never be the same. Fonz and Ronnie Moe heard the shots but didn't make anything out of it as they made their way back to Meka's building. As soon as they stepped in they saw Donte sprawled out. "What the fuck!!" Ronnie Moe shouts. Meka was beating Stoney against his chest and face screaming, while he still held the gauge. They didn't know what to do for real, I mean Donte was they man and so was Stoney, eventhough he was younger they'd all grew up together. Reality kicked in and their first instinct was to take Donte to the hospital.

"Move!!" Fonz screamed. "C'mon Donte be strong my nigga you a soldier this shit ain't nothing to you." Fonz was sitting in the backseat holding his head still and putting pressure on his chest wounds with an old T-shirt. Ronnie Moe was driving like a bat out of hell.

"Man what the fuck going on? Fuck this shit dog, Stoney gotta go, I put that on everything. I don't give a fuck." Ronnie Moe was talking in riddles mostly out of anger and emotions. He was the closest to Donte out of all the fellas. They were together so much, you'd think they were attached to the hip. It was easy for him

34

to choose sides instantly. Detroit Receiving Hospital was right around the corner on Mack Ave. and St. Antoine, so they made it there in about one minute flat. They both rushed Donte in leaving the doors open and the car running. The whole situation looked like the scene from Menace II Society when Kane was shot and everybody was going nuts. The difference being though, this ain't no movie, this is real life. Donte wouldn't survive like Kane did and died before they even put his back on the stretcher. Fonz and Ronnie Moe went ballistic on the doctors, but it was nothing they could do. It was too late, a lost cause. Donte was gone.

Chapter 4

["I got mouths to feed, until they put flowers on me, and kiss my cold cheek, chicks crying like I was Kocheeks, tombstone read, he was holding no leaks."] Rome sat in the backseat of Ski's S600 while Jay-Z blared from the speakers.

"Rome! Rome!!"

"Huh?" Shane called Rome from the passenger seat snapping him out of the zone Jay-Z had him in.

"You hungry?"

"Oh yeah, yeah I'm hungry."

"Alright we bout to stop at Capers and get some carry-out."

"Alright bet."

"You getting some pussy yet little nigga?" Ski asks Rome with a grin on his face. Ski was heavy in the game, he had what you called real clientele. You wouldn't catch him behind the wheel if it wasn't nothing foreign. He went to his connect funeral 4 years ago and met this older broad from Miami. He was 21 at the time with a fly mouthpiece and his hustle hand was platinum. His trick bill was high and he loved the ladies. Come to find out this time he hit the goldmine, ol girl was the plug. She started dumping birds on him five and ten at a time and he ain't looked back since.

"You heard me little nigga?"

"Oh yeah man, what you think?" Rome looked at him like he was crazy.

"I don't know, that's why I'm asking."

"Yeah I'm doing a little something. I'll be 14 next month, I couldn't turn 14 a virgin."

"Yeah alright, don't be acting scared next time I bring some hoes around then."

"Man my nephew not scared of no females." Shane was getting back in the car with the food in his hand.

Oh, did I forget to mention Ski kept a bad chick with him. All types of females, exotic, professional women, bourgeoisie hoodrats, whatever the case they all had something in common, they were beautiful.

"Hey Rome you going back to the house?" Shane asked.

"Naw drop me off on Concord St." Rome wanted to make himself look like something and stunt on Dana getting dropped off in the Benz. A few minutes later they pulled up, he was salty Dana wasn't on the porch, but he got out anyway. He figured he'd catch Dana alone and see whatsup. He knew he had a better chance alone with her cause females act funny around company. Her grandma wasn't home because her Buick was gone, plus it was Sunday and that meant Bingo day. Rome crept around to her bedroom after not getting an answer from the front door. What he seen shocked him eventhough it shouldn't have. Donnie was on top of Dana humping away. He couldn't get mad because that wasn't his girl, but he did feel some type of way. How she gone be playing him on the pussy but be giving Donnie some? To make matters worse, his man didn't even tell him he was still fucking her.

Maybe this was his first time since she took their virginity though. Yeah it probably was, or who knows. Man fuck that bitch, she a slut anyway. All these thoughts crossed Rome's mind as he walked home. He was so deep in the zone, he almost got hit by a car while crossing the street. He kept trying to tell himself it wasn't that serious. It took him about thirty minutes to make a five to ten minute walk. He looked to see the usual crowd in front of the house, but this time it was a bunch of sad and long faces. A bunch of empty bottles and low conversation. It seemed like no one was paying attention to Rome and those who were, was looking right through him. He walked in the house to see his moms sitting at the kitchen table with her face in her palms sniffling. When she raised her face, her eyes were red and watery. He looked up and Ms. Patti's were the same.

"Ma! Ma!" Rome shouted while shaking her shoulders. "Grandma what's going on?"

"Donte...Donte he dead baby. He gone!!" she screamed.

Rome teared up instantly, he tried to hold it but eventually let it go. A lot of outsiders despised Donte for his "I don't give a fuck" attitude and his careless behavior. To those who was close to him it was genuine love. Rome was close to Donte, not only was it his cousin, but one of his favorite oldheads. He reminisced on how Donte took him to his first football practice and made him sign up, or made him put on boxing gloves and box the young cats down the street.

Donte was the type of person who made you have heart when you didn't have none. It could be looked at different ways, an instigator, motivator, whatever you wanna call it. At fourteen Rome felt like he wanted to avenge his death.

"Fuck Stoney and fuck the hood!!" he shouted to himself.

For the rest of the oldheads it was a weird vibe outside. You had those who wanted to ride for Donte, some who was with Stoney, and some who just didn't give a fuck. You know how it is when the hood lose a soldier. Niggas drink a couple bottles, act all mad, then once the adrenaline wear off, its back to the basics. A couple days later life goes on, its fucked up but that's how it is.

On the other side of town, Stoney was hiding out in one of his brothers stash houses off Fenkell Ave on the Westside. No one had seen him since the incident. Soon as they left the hospital, Fonz and Ronnie Moe went right back to the projects to find Meka in the same spot crying with the kids. The gauge was sitting on the floor next to her, but Stoney was gone. Ronnie Moe was so heated, he spazzed out and put his 4-5 to Meka's head.

"Where the fuck he at?"

"I don't know, what the fuck is wrong with you!" Meka responded shakily.

39

"Calm down dog, you tripping, Meka loved that nigga," Fonz said while easing the 4-5 out of his hand.

Five days had passed and Stoney still had on the same clothes pacing the floor on his third straight pint of Seagram's Gin. He didn't care what he was drinking as long as it was strong. Only a couple of the fellas knew where this house was located. Those were the ones he had faith in enough to know they wouldn't come looking for him. He had mixed feelings, he did grow up with the nigga. He fooled himself into thinking he did the right thing because Donte constantly abused his sister, but in all actuality, it made things worse. He'd just taken his nephews and nieces father away. Two negatives never equal a positive, but the logic in the hood always say otherwise.

Back on the eastside, Meka was over her mother house on Houston Whittier and Gratiot Ave. She knew the family knew where her brother was, but was keeping if from her. Meka wouldn't put her brother's life in danger, but she wanted him to pay for his actions for taking her kids father. It wasn't fair to them she felt. To Meka's advantage the walls and floors were thin in her mother's house. She was upstairs in her old room playing sleep. Her older sister Toni was downstairs on the phone gossiping with one of her girlfriends, she slipped up and said Stoney's location in more than one instant. Little did she know, she gave Meka exactly what she needed. Meka left, went to the payphone and made the hardest phone call of her life. "Hello this is the 9th precinct..........

Chapter 5

"RING!   RING!!" (phone ringing) "Hello?" Donnie answered the phone sounding energetic.

"Whatup doe?" Rome greeted him.

"What's the deal my nigga you ready to get this money tonight?"

"Shit man shit fucked up."

"What's up dog, talk to me?"

"Donte gone man, Stoney killed him."

"What! When? What happened?"

"I don't know I found out the night before last."

"Damn, man I'm on my way over." Donnie was at Rome's house five minutes later.

"Damn nigga what you was speed walking?" Rome stated.

"Cut it out, you alright my nigga?"

"Yeah I'm good it's not the first time we lost a soldier you know."

"Man Donte was like an uncle to me." Don said while shaking his head.

"I already know," said Rome but it appeared his mind was elsewhere.

"We might as well get blasted dog." Donnie pulled an open pint of Martell out his back pocket. "It's already cracked but it's enough to get us there."

"Fuck it, Rome snatched the bottle out of Donnie's hand, almost guzzling the whole thing.

"Slow down dog." Don told him trying to grab the bottle from his lips.

Him and Don were upstairs passing the bottle back and forth smoking an el. Rome said fuck it and gave in to the weed. Tupac could be heard blasting in the background. ["How many brothers fell victim to the streets, rest in peace young nigga, there's a heaven for a 'G', be a lie if I told you that I never thought of death, my niggas, we the last ones left, but life goes on."] Suddenly, Tupac was fading out snapping Don out of his zone.

"Fuck you doing dog?" Don snapped. Rome cut the music down.

"Hold on dog, I almost forgot, why you ain't tell me you was still fucking Dana?"

"What you talking about?" Don was trying to play dumb-founded.

"Oh so you gone play your mans like that, nigga I seen you fucking her Sunday. I creep around to her window and I see you humping away, speedy gonzalez." Rome said with a drunk laugh.

"Aw nigga fuck that bitch, I was gone tell you."

"Whatever dog, you catching feelings that's why you ain't tell me."

"Naw she told me not to tell you that's why I ain't say nothing."

"What!! Oh so we putting hoes before us now?" Rome was getting excited raising his voice.

"Yeah, yeah you right, money over bitches. M.O.B." Don confirmed.

"But hold up, what was you doing over there, you was trying to do the same thing," Don said smiling just catching on. Rome couldn't do nothing but smile. "Yeah that's what I thought, that's off limits now though playboy, I got her in a headlock.

Outside Jake was pulling up with his older cousin Omar driving. ["Lyrically I'm suppose to represent, I'm not only a client, I'm the player president."] Biggie could be heard from the sounds of his old school T-top Monte SS. You couldn't tell him nothing, flip flop paint sitting on 18's. The average hood nigga, who thought he was killing them, but really wasn't doing nothing, didn't know how to wait his turn.

"Hey man, good looking out," Jake told his cousin as they were pulling up. "Let me take the rest of that blunt with me."

"Man get your young crackhead ass out the car. You should of stayed in Southwest with me and got some real money." Omar responded.

"I told you, me and my mans had something up." Omar wasn't trying to hear it, if it was up to him

Jake would of sat in the spot all night rolling for next to nothing.

"What yall bout to do, bust some windows out or something?" Omar asked, amusing himself.

"Fuck out of here, we trying to eat!" Jake slammed the door before Omar could respond.

"Whatup doe? You ready to eat or what?"

Don shouted while holding the raggedy 2-5 as Jake walked through the door.

"Man yall niggas drunk as a skunk, what yall trying to go to jail?" Jake took notice instantly.

"Man whatever we good."

Jake stood there shaking his head as they filled each other in.

Chapter 6

"OOOH Ahh! Uh Huh, Uh huh just like that baby. Take your time you gone get it. Open your mouth wider and tuck your teeth."

"Odell it's too big," Dana says with the puppy dog face.

"You doing good baby."

Dana was getting her first lesson in head game 101. Odell bought her some low top Gucci loafers and a Coogi dress for her as a birthday gift. Funny thing it wasn't her B-day for another six months. In return he told her he just wanted her to kiss it. That turned into a lick, suck, now he had her going.

"Ohh shit baby your mouth feel so good, you gone make me cum." Odell was in ectasy. "Your mouth so warm. What you doing? Dana why you stop?"

"Look!"

"Oh."

Odell's little cousin Willie was knocking on the passenger side window.

"Fuck you want little nigga?" Odell says pissed.

"Damn, what you doing in there dog? Anyway ol boy say he right around the corner, he bout to pull up."

"Alright here I come."

Odell was at one of his homes on Wade & Dickerson. He didn't live there, just one of the places he did business. He let his younger cousin Willie live there rent free, all he had to do was sit there and make the transactions.

"Baby I be right back ok?"

"Damn you just gone leave me out here in the car?" Dana wasn't feeling that.

"I'm just gone be a couple minutes."

"I'm coming in!"

"Baby chill you don't need to be around this shit." Odell was spinning her like he really cared, but he just didn't want her in his business. Shit young girls could be slick too, was the thoughts crossing his mind.

Soon as he walked in the house, he got to complaining. A weed smoke mixed with funk aroma filled the air.

"Man you need to clean this muthafucka up."

"It's all good, I'm a have dopefiend Brenda clean it up first thing in the morning, Willie responded while picking up empty weed baggies and beer bottles off the floor.

"What you say dude wanted, 4 ½ right?" Odell asked.

"Naw he called back and said he wanted nine."

"Holdup, I left the other half in the car." On his way out the door, it looked like a raid in progress. He slammed the door fast before he was spotted.

"Ohh shit!!"

Three black narco cars were outside with his truck blocked in. Dana was stretched out looking like she just seen a ghost. Two of the narcs were questioning her while three more were searching the truck. Whose truck is this? How old are you? Is it anything in here we should know about? The questions were coming too fast.

Before she could get an answer out they were asking her something else. At a young age Dana was hood to the core, but the intimidation role the officers were playing, was starting to take its toll. Her eyes were starting to water and her hands were shaking. It was like a shark tasting blood that was all they needed to see to keep them going.

"Uh Oh!" "Jackpot." "Hey Peters, look what we got here?"

Officer Jacobs was black, husky and about 6'5 245lbs. It was only his sixth month on the force and he had already been transferred to the narcotics division. He looked like he could of played linebacker for the NFL's elite. This was one of the strategies of the DPD. They try to get the biggest, toughest looking guys to work on the narcotics task force. They knew most of the workers in the drug houses were young and scary. There look along with the scare tactics made them feel like it would make them easier to crack.

Officer Jacobs lifted up 4 ½ ounces of soft he found wrapped in some dirty clothes in the trunk. He was grinning from ear to ear as he walked up to Dana. Odell was pacing back and forth inside the house.

"Damn I hope they don't find that shit," he said talking to himself. He didn't wanna keep looking out the blinds making himself hot.

"Now we can make this easy or do this the hard way." Officer Peters asked Dana. "We know the driver of this vehicle is in one of these houses. We know these drugs don't belong to you. Shit, you don't look no older than 17. Am I correct?

"Hmmm Hmmm." Dana shook her head sniffling.

Peters continued his ranting. "We know who Odell is, now just make it easy for the both of us and tell us which house he went in. We'll kick in every muthafuckin door on this block if we have to."

That was a lie, most of the narcos in this area were lazy and crooked. They probably was just gone process a half ounce and sell the rest to one of the dealers in the hood at a discount.

"So, what its gone be, I don't have all night." Peters asked giving Dana eye contact.

Odell still refused to look out the window, he was shook. The public say all hustlers are cowards, well he was one of them that lived up to it.

"I ain't going to jail over no fluke shit. That little bitch better keep her mouth shut." Odell told Willie while shaking his head back and forth.

"Man that young girl gone crack, I don't know why you keep fucking with them young hoes." "Matter of fact I ain't bout to sit in here and wait on them to come, I'm out." Willie said while getting up heading towards the back door.

"Sit your ass down nigga, they watching every house in the radius." Odell raised his voice with fire in his eyes.

"Man they ain't watching the back."

"Fuck all that chill!"

"So, what its gone be, I don't have all night." Peters said impatiently. Odell had her steaming, she wanted to point to the house he was in so bad. Even a ten year old in the hood knew, when it came to police, you kept your mouth shut and didn't know anything. Somehow in her mind, she felt her loyalty would pay off.

"I don't know what you talking bout." "Leave me the fuck alone!" Dana's fear transformed to anger.

"Oh, so you wanna play hardball huh?" Jacobs! "Cuff her young ass up, take her down for a minute and see how she feel then." And call the tow-truck for this vehicle. This gone be a little harder than I thought, Peters contemplated in his head.

Chapter 7

"Alright man yall gone have to let me hold the pistol cause yall too drunk." Jake was starting to feel like he should of stayed in Southwest with his cousin. Don wasn't having it though.

"Nigga this my pistol and my lick, its 2:30 in the morning let's get up out of here." Rome high was wearing off and he felt where Jake was coming from.

"Yeah dog, let Jake hold the mag down, you on some super amp shit."

"Man fuck yall niggas! Donte gone! Money over bitches! I'm trying to eat! If yall scared, get a dog!" Don was just shouting, talking in riddles, saying a bunch of shit that didn't make sense, clear signs of being drunk.

"Man let him hold the mag down or I ain't going." Rome spoke up.

"Fuck you, we don't need you nigga!"

"I ain't going either." Jake cosigned Rome.

"Ah ha! Ha! Ha! Ah ha! Ha! Ha!" Don just burst out laughing handing the 2-5 to Jake, dude was tripping.

It was about a five minute walk to Bellevue and Mack to get to the warehouse the Rave party was being held. The line was almost around the block as usual. Rave parties were held in the hood like every blue moon. They weren't held for the people in the hood though. The warehouses or recreation centers in the hood were just convenient for the hosts of the party. It was a lot of space for cheap and they can go all the way to the next morning as needed. The consequences were costly though, the hood needed they share, by any means.

Most of the clientele for the Raves were suburbanites or the punk rock type with the spiked hair. They loved to get high though, and all the local small time hustlers were swarming with weed, cocaine, pills or whatever you needed. People was even posted in vacant lots with $10 parking signs like they owned them. They fell right into the trap though, cause soon as their cars were parked and the coast was clear, it was a wrap. They would break into the cars and steal everything from the sound systems to the car even. Niggas was starving and they had to eat. Everybody wanted a piece and at age 14, Rome, Don, and Jake needed their share.

"Alright first group we see that look like they working with something, we on them." "Get that shit over with while it's still a lot of traffic and nobody paying attention." Don was giving instructions but it was going in one ear and out the other.

"Listen man, you tripping we gone lay out here behind these cars and catch them slipping on the way in or the way out." "In and out real fast just follow my lead." Jake said seriously.

Neither one of their logic made much sense, but you might as well add that to the list, cause standing out there bare face didn't either. After ten minutes of just sitting, Rome came up with a idea.

"Look, Momo doing the parking, so I'm a tell him to whistle when he see something sweet." Rome broke the silence and they all agreed. Not more than five minutes passed before Momo was whistling.

"Fucking hey man, this shit rocks. Rude Jude knows how to jam dude. Hey look at that rack on her, she hot." The three white boys never saw it coming as they closed the door on the souped up Honda Civic. Jake hopped out of nowhere like jack in the box.

"Lay the fuck down real slow!"

"Oh shit!!" "Oh my God!" The white boys panicked as they fell to their feet.

"Lay flat on your stomach and we gone make this quick and easy." "My man gone get that shit off yall neck and out yall pockets."

"See Tom, I told you we should of left earlier, who the fuck comes to a party at 3 in the morning? This is a rave stupid, that's what time the party gets going." The white boys whispered under their breath.

"Jackpot!" Don shouted. "We got a roley!"

"That's my father's watch fuck! You guys won't get away with this, its undercovers all over the place."

"Shut the fuck up, yall doing a little too much talking." Crack!! Jake smacked Tom upside his head with the butt of the pistol. Aw! Aw! His head was gushing.

"C'mon we out." Rome was ready, the job was done.

52

"Bitch ass nigga." Jake shouted while kicking the white boy in the head repeatedly. "Listen when grown folks talking to you." Jake was over doing it.

"C'mon dog, you gone get us knocked."

"Man fuck these crackers." Jake said with spit dripping from his lips.

"Oh my gosh, look at that line." "I know Jamie, I'm not waiting in that." Two white girls with piercings everywhere visible were approaching.

"Jake somebody coming man, we out, you on some other shit." Rome said while pulling his shirt. Don was sitting there with the goods in his pocket the whole time enjoying that shit. While Jake was in the zone, all three of them took off running clumsily. Jake was running with the gun in his hand out in the open. They were so reckless none of them noticed it. Luckily the route back to Rome's house was all back streets. You'd think they was competing for the 100 yard dash as fast as these boys were moving. Don was the first to slow down.

"Slow down, we good now, I don't wanna drop none of this shit." Everybody else fell in place. It was about four in the morning as they walked into Rome's house. Soon as they walked in Debra was walking and fidgeting, looking out windows and fixing up things that didn't need to be fixed. Rome knew she was high.

"Boy where yall been? And why yall sweating? Uh huh, yall up to something," she commented.

"Ma we ain't up to nothing, we just coming from Donnie's house." Rome said irritated.

53

"Yeah whatever, yall hungry?"

"Naw we good."

"Well, I'm bout to make a run right quick, don't wake your grandmother up." Debra said on her way out.

They all sat down in the living room while Don emptied his pockets.

"Man, we only got like $1,100 in cash, but we got this Rolex and Turkish Link."

"Man that shit might not even be real, let me see that." Jake was always thinking negative.

"It ain't nothing we can take it up to the Goldmine and see whatsup in the morning." "Jake you almost got us knocked on that extra shit too." Rome couldn't wait to get that out since Jake always thought he knew it all and had it under control.

"Like my cousin Omar say, everytime we do something we gotta send a message. Make a muthafucka think twice about coming at you." Said Jake trying to contain a laugh.

"Man these was some white boys, what the fuck is you talking bout?" All three of them burst out laughing.

"Plus I was mad when I seen they didn't have that much."

Truthfully there was really no explanation, that's just how Jake was. Loved to be in the middle of something, in the midst of the fire. He wanted to get shit started and finish it. Jake and Don eventually dozed off, Rome just sat up in a daze. His mother still wasn't back yet. Her situation bothered him, but he felt helpless. She had to help herself first, what could he do? It wasn't like he could go to every drug dealer in the City and say don't sell to my moms. Impossible. He sat on the couch and realized he was sitting on his mother's bed. He felt what he called home was a shack. The stain filled walls with cobwebs in the corner. Every room cluttered with junk including the kitchen. The carpet was so old it felt and looked like brillo pad. Even at a young age, he knew this wasn't living. This was his motivation, slowly but surely he needed a way out by any means.

Chapter 8

Dana sat in the cold pissy cell feeling helpless and stupid. Narcotics Officer Peters spent three hours trying to get her to sign a statement. To no avail, she didn't crack, but now she was having second thoughts. By now, she figured Odell would of posted her bail, but he was a no show. She didn't know how long she could sit on the hard slab of concrete or put up with the smell. Let alone the voices or screams of the other prisoners. She was suppose to be at the 9th, but they took her to the 7th precinct out of spite. This was the grimiest and oldest precinct in the City. The cells were never cleaned and most of the phones were broken. One of the female officers gave her three phone calls because she felt bad for her, right now, she was on her fourth.

"C'mon c'mon answer the phone." Dana whispered while holding the phone. "Hello you have reached the automated voice mailbox of "O," please leave a message after the tone." "Damn!" Dana snapped after getting the voicemail for the umpteenth time.

"Girl he ain't answered the other four or five times, he not gone answer now." It's not no coincidence, he not answering the phone all of a sudden. You don't have nobody else to call, cause I'm not letting you out here no more. The female officer knew the drill, she seen it play out too many times. If she had the $1,500 to spare, she'd bail her out herself.

"Damn where this nigga at?" Dana screamed while breaking down crying at the same time. "I can't believe this shit. I ain't going back to that cell." Dana was scratching her arms up and down shaking.

"Listen baby, you sure you don't have no one else to call. My supervisor on his way back, I can't give you but one more call, then that's it. Look call your grandmother, she gone be mad for awhile, but she at least will come get you."

"No I can't!"

"Call your mother then." The officer was persistent.

"My mother died five years ago. She was in and out of jail and she always say I'm gone end up just like her. I call her, I won't hear the end of it." Dana stood there contemplating, trying to figure out something. "Shoot, shoot let me think, naw they won't be able to do nothing. Fuck it, 9…,2, 3,….2, 6,…6, 2."

Chapter 9

The fellas were feeling themselves walking out of the Goldmine Pawn Shop on Mt. Elliot & Gratiot. They all had big Kool-Aid smiles on they face. The clerk appraised the Rolex and the Turkish Link, confirming it was real. Seeing how young they were, the clerk saw an opportunity. She gave them $3,000 for both of the pieces, when the Rolex was at least worth $6,500 by itself at half price. Being impatient and anxious, Jake, Don and Rome took the money willingly.

"Girl why you do them little boys like that," the clerk light skinned co-worker asked.

"They had it coming, shit I ain't never felt sorry for no sucker. You feel me," she said laughing as she slapped high-fivers with her co-worker.

Jake was disturbed by the whole situation. Man $1,500 a piece, we could of did way better than that."

"It's better than what we started with." Rome continued.

Don was elated, "I'm bout to go to Eastland and get geared up. Whatsup yall with me?"

"Let's stop at my crib first," said Rome. Soon as they reached the house Rome's little sister Carrie was at the front door like she couldn't wait until Rome came home.

"Rome somebody keep calling here collect. It keep saying from jail, I don't know what to do, so I keep hanging up." Carrie talked fast naturally even at 9 years old.

"Where moms at?"

"She went to the store, grandma upstairs sleep."

"You hungry?" Rome asked his little sister. He always made sure she was straight before he left the house. "Here, call the coney island and order you something while I change my clothes, I'm bout to go to the mall.

Carrie dialed the number to the coney island eagerly. Soon as the phone started ringing, the line started clicking. "Hello, Grandy's Coney Island, May I take your order please?" "Hold on my line clicking." Sure. Carrie clicked over making the flat tire sound, irritated.

"Hello?" "You have a collect call from Dana, from the Wayne County Jail, to accept....." Carrie put the phone down and immediately yelled for her brother. Rome!! Rome!!!

"What!"

"The phone, these people calling again, you want it?"

"Give it here Carrie, why you ain't just ignore it. You know this the first place niggas call when they get locked up." Rome said hello, just as the recording was being repeated. His mouth dropped soon as he heard Dana's name. He accepted the call more out of curiosity than caring for her well-being.

"Hello? Hello?"

"Whatsup."

"Rome that's you?"

"Yeah, what the fuck you doing calling here from jail, what's going on?"

"I couldn't call nowhere else. You gotta help me, I been in here three days. Odell nowhere to be found. They just bought me downtown to the County, my bail $15,000, ten percent $1,500."

"Hold on slow down girl damn. Why you calling here? Why you ain't call Don?" Rome said sarcastically.

"Boy stop playing, you know his phone cut off. Anyway Rome I'm serious, I need yall help." "Ask all them niggas that be around your house. See what yall can do, I'll pay yall back." It was all or nothing, Dana had her sympathetic voice on and all that.

"Man you talking crazy, Don over here, I'm a put him on the phone. Hold on. Don, your girl on the phone." Rome shouted outside interrupting him and Jake's arguing.

Don ran in the house, snatched the phone and walked to the back of the house as if he had something to hide. "Hello?"

"Don I need you A.S.A.P."

"Where you at?"

"I'm downtown at the County, my bail $1,500, I need yall to put it together. I'll pay it back, you know I can't call nobody else. I'll pay it back." Dana was talking so fast it sounded like she was mumbling.

"Hold on girl, slow down damn." "What happened?" Don asked frustrated.

"Man I'll explain that later. Can you come get me?" The female officer was signaling Dana that she didn't have much time.

"Yeah I got you baby, give me a minute to put something together."

"Don don't lie to me."

"I got you baby, no bullshit." Soon as Don hung up the phone, Rome was in his face. "Damn dog, how many teeth I got?" Don said laughing, while being sarcastic, you all in my grill.

"So you told her you was bailing her out huh? Damn you must really love her, you gone use your whole $1,500. I'd leave that bitch for dead just like Odell did." Rome spoke his mind.

"Naw man that ain't cool." Don said seriously. Don was working off feelings, but he didn't wanna show it. Rome knew it too, but his respect for his man led him not to speak on it. Plus he didn't wanna seem jealous.

"I need yall to help me man, give me $400 a piece and I'll come up with the rest. That way I'll still have a couple dollars to work with."

"Man, you tripping." Rome wasn't feeling that idea.

"C'mon dog, she said she'll pay us back."

"How she gone do that?"

"You know she be stashing that little money niggas be giving her." Don was pleading his case.

"Man whatever dog, I got you, but you know Jake ain't gone be with that shit."

"I ain't gone be with what?" Jake walked in on the conversation coming from the store, eating a .99 cent bag of chips with two swishers in his back pocket. "Be with what dog?"

"Dana need us to help bail her out. Her bail $1,500." Don looked at Jake like he was shocked, when he had no reason to be.

"So, why you telling me, she ain't giving me no pussy. Yall got it." Jake responded.

"C'mon dog she gone pay us back."

"Damn Don you putting up a fit for your baby huh? Here fuck it, there go $300, but I need mine back no bullshit. Don I'm holding you responsible, sucker for love."

"Shutup nigga you gone get your bread back." Don said smiling.

Chapter 10

Fonz and Tone was on the block shooting they regular. Drinking, talking shit, and swallowing spit. A couple of the other fellas was in the background speaking on last night's escapade.

"Yeah, so I tell the bitch to bring her friend with her cause ain't no reason for her to miss out on all this. The light skinned one laughed and then hit me with, we don't get down like that." Ski was in the middle of one of his stories. "I'm like your mind in the gutter, what tip you on, so she start smiling...."

Ski story was cut short and everyone else who was talking heads turned. Tires screeched as Geno's 740IL turned the corner. Geno was Stoney's older brother, he was plugged, in other words, he had a lot of connects. He know how to utilize them, but he came up back in '92'. He took a group of hungry niggas out to Redding, PA and took over. When they came home everybody went to the lot and cashed out, he ain't looked back since. Right now he was under the impression somebody gave his little brother up. Not realizing family is the ones you gotta watch the closest. Geno pulls up recklessly with the car parked sideways, he hops out with the doors still open. Eyes bloodshot red, AK-47 in his hand in broad daylight on some "I don't give a fuck shit."

"What's the deal, I was always bought up you hold court in the streets. Yall want war, we settle it like men." Tone was the first to speak.

"Fuck you talking bout Geno?"

"Nigga they got my brother down there on an anonymous tip. Somebody singing round this bitch."

"C'mon nigga put the K down, you know how we was brought up." Fonz spoke up. "Now if you wanna take it there, we can, but put that up unless you gone use it. You ain't the only nigga with choppers."

"Yeah alright, the streets gone start talking soon, yall know where I'm at," was Geno's last words as he hopped in his whip and sped off recklessly.

Rome: "Ok, ok, hold up, hold up Rio, I agreed to let you tell our story but you venturing off topic too much. I already went against the grain by letting you tell the story, but if you gone tell it, tell it right. The book called "Coming of Age," this is me & my man's story, or basically my story. Yeah I love the oldheads but all that shit they went through is irrelevant."

Rio (author) "Man that's meant to show your experiences and surroundings and how they affected you. It's all a part of "Coming of Age," what made you."

Rome: "Man fuck all that."

Rio: "What you mean, this my book."

Rome: "Look chill I got this. Ladies and Gentlemen, to my dear readers. As you my know, my name is Jerome Wilson a.k.a. Rome. You know a little about me so far but I must intervene. I mean Rio, no offense, but this is your first book and its showing. You leaving out key points and plus you starting to bore me. Like for instance, for all the ladies reading this I wanna give you a visual. I'm about 6'1 dark skin, but not too

64

black about 200 lbs, low hair cut with deep waves and I always been fly."

Rio: "That's a lie." (author interrupts)

Rome: "Man, quit hating, but anyway not always but this is when things start to look up. I mean we was still fucked up, but I felt like this was a turning point. Let's get back to it as told by me, Rio sit back for a minute, I got this."

Rio: "Man you can fuck up a wet dream."

Rome: "Shutup dude. Alright, where were we? Yeah Geno did pull up on the block with that dumb shit. I was in the house when it all went down. Even as a spring chicken, as my O.G. Black use to call me, I knew it was a certain way, you was supposed to go about things. I knew the difference between being tough and being stupid, and that was just reckless. I don't know why Rio even decided to put that in the book. Anyway, back to me and my peoples. It was around 97', 98', I was 14 or 15 at the time and it was a transition. Like my man Hov said, "It's time to transform you Boys 2 Men like day care." Man Dana had my man Don nose wide open. That nigga mind was gone. I mean the pussy was good, but by this time, I had got some more and I was over it. Honestly though, I gotta admit she was a stallion. At 17, she put a lot of grown women to shame. Light skinned, but not too light. Her complexion was one of a kind, sort of like light caramel. It made her look like she always had on makeup when she never wore it. Bow-legged stance by nature. Titties stand up like they were implants, thick in all the right places. I know what yall thinking, how I'm a talk about my man girl like that. But shit, we family, plus when we say

65

M.O.B. we really mean that shit. Anyway, I'm getting off topic."

Rio: "Yes you are!"

Rome: "Chill Rio, I got this. We ran through that little money quick after Don talked us into bailing Dana out. We was supposed to cop us some weed. You know try to flip our money. Man we blew that shit, went to the mall got fresh for the fireworks at Hart Plaza. Yeah, those were the days, the fireworks and the festivals downtown. Throw on your best fit and see who could get the most numbers. Jake was the only one who followed through with the plan of flipping his money. He went straight to his cousin Omar because he knew he could kill two birds with one stone. Whatever he copped he'd also have a place to get rid of it. He bought him one of them cheap nines made by Hi-Point. He was trying to come up. Jake mindstate was ahead of his time, I gotta give it to him. At the end of the day, he still got played out his money. Omar taxed that nigga $175 for a quarter ounce. He had to cut the rocks so big to keep up with Omar clientele he only make like twenty dollars, shit was ridiculous. Jake was riding Don about not paying that bail money back, but Don had other plans. I gotta respect how he pulled it off."

Rio: "Alright let me take it from here."

Rome: "Damn, I was just getting warmed up."

Rio: "Man how you gone tell everybody else story too!"

Rome: "It's from my point of view."

Rio: "It's my book!!!"

Rome: "Yeah, yeah alright, I'll be back though."

Chapter 11

["Forever my lady, it's like a dream…, I'm holding you close and keeping you warm."] Jodeci is being played softly in the background. Don swore he had game. Dana had been staying at his house for the past week. Only reason his mother allowed it was because of the money he was feeding her. He always felt like he needed to be the man of the house, he helped out but never really financially. That all changed once they robbed them white boys and pulled some petty stick-ups after that.

"Baby how many times you gone play that song," Dana says as she lay in the bed in one of Don's t-shirts with nothing on underneath.

"That's my song baby, plus you know that's my message to you. Me and you forever." Don was gassing her, she really didn't know how he felt.

"Whatever, niggas always talking good when they want some pussy. No, no I won't fall for that again." Dana says with a smirk on her face.

"Shutup, plus I already beat that thing up a couple times, you can't handle no more."

"Whatever, you did alright, you not all that." Dana responded. "Baby you know what I been thinking," she said while rubbing his back. "I already know when I go back home my grandmother probably gone kick me out."

"Not if you hurry up and go back home, and plus all you gotta do is graduate and you good," Don interrupted.

68

"Shit I done missed two months already, plus them hoes up at Kettering (H.S.) be hating too much. But like I was saying baby, we can get our own apt, get us a whip. I can go to school and get my beautician license."

"Yeah and where the money gone come from for all this."

"Damn boy let me finish, yall can rob Odell. Ain't no use in running around and keep doing all this petty shit. I been to two of his stash houses and he think I don't know. I be playing the dumb role, but I know he got a lot of shit in there. Everytime we stop at one of them, another car pull up, go in the same house and come out. It's always a nice whip too, Benzes, Mitsubishis, some of them be nicer than his."

"But I thought he was done with you since that shit went down," Don asked with his eyebrows raised.

"Man he been blowing my phone up trying to apologize. All I gotta do is say the word and he'll be over here. You know I got that snapper." Dana was on a roll, feeling herself. "Baby I been thinking bout this all morning. Whatsup yall with it? Yall always talking this money over bitches and how yall need some bread shit."

"Yeah you know I'm with it, but how I know you not still feeling dude."

Dana cut him off before he could finish. "Man fuck that nigga!! I can't believe you even asked me that."

69

"Alright calm down, I'm a holler at them and we gone put something together. You gone have to hook up with him a couple times first, so it won't be obvious."

Don knew Dana still had feelings for Odell. She was just reacting off emotions talking reckless. He figured he might as well capitalize off it. Shit this was a meal ticket, exactly what they had been waiting on.

Rome: "Man you making me regret I let you tell our story. You boring than a muthafucka."

Rio: "Rome you can't just keep cutting in like that."

Rome: "Man real niggas do what they want, bitch niggas do what they can."

Rio: "Rome what are you talking bout, what you buzzin or something?"

Rome: "Nah, but for real listen though. I remember when Don called me about hitting a lick on Odell. I'm not gone lie at first I was like how we gone pull that off. I was 15 at the time he called. I was naive at the time, like Nas said "I thought Jordan's and a gold chain was living it up." I stayed fresh, kept a couple dollars in my pocket, and I thought that was all to it. At first I thought Dana was on some bullshit, but Don convinced me otherwise. I really don't know the word I'm looking for, but he could convince a person anything. He could make a Harvard graduate believe he was stupid.

Our plan wasn't foolproof, but it was good enough to get the job done. This was the first real robbery. We had done a lot of petty stick-ups in the

70

past, me and Don would spend most of our money on gear. Maybe buy a couple ounces of weed or something, quarter or eightball here and there, but nothing major. We'd always end up with what we started with or if not, maybe just $50 or $60 more.

But as I would learn later on in life, it's not what you make, but how fast you move it. Jake spent a lot of time in Southwest with Omar. Omar was basically playing him, but he still made good use of his money. When we told him about the robbery, he was all for it. In fact his exact response was "Bout time that bitch made herself useful." He said he was bringing the guns and it was a go."

Rio (author): "I'm taking it from here Rome. We keep messing with you, we won't get published."

Rome: "We will if you pick up the pace."

Rio: "Chill man I got it from here."

Don was ecstatic, last night he felt like he was 12 and it was Christmas Eve. Only difference he was 15 and this was like Christmas to him, he considered this the big ticket. Him being young and not knowing any better, he thought 30 or 40 grand would get him and his fam out the hood for good. The plan was all laid out. The past couple weeks Dana had been playing Odell real close. He even got comfortable and started letting her inside the houses. He felt guilty for not bailing her out and Dana was using that to her advantage. They went out to eat every night and tore down all the malls. Dana never faced the music and her grandma eventually kicked her out. So, after every escapade she had with Odell, she would get dropped off over Don's house.

Coming in with bags and carry out from some of the finest restaurants around the City. She even started giving Don money to give to his mother. Don felt himself getting jealous. He kept his eye on the bigger picture though, Dana's feelings were growing for Odell. She tried to hide it, but it was written all over her face.

She was acting lackadaisical about the robbery, putting it off as long as she could. She felt like she didn't need it anymore. Odell had her feeling like she was living the high life, Gucci this, Prada that.

"Tonight it's going down man, no more procrastinating," Don said with his face frowned up.

"You sure, I told you he bout to re-up in a couple days," Dana said. She had been using that same excuse for the last couple days.

"Man ain't nobody trying to hear that shit, we done put this shit off long enough. We got everything set up. Rome already at his house waiting with the car. Odell on his way to pick you up right?"

"Yeah."

"Lift your head up, what's wrong with you. You know what you gotta do right?" Don asked with fire in his eyes.

"Don just make sure yall don't kill him alright."

"Girl chill ain't nobody gone kill your little boyfriend."

"I'm just saying that shit gone cause problems."

"Girl, we know what we doing. Now tell me what you gotta do before I get up out of here."

"I know," Dana responded.

"Let me hear it!" Don was on point.

"I leave my purse in the car on purpose. I start kissing on him and getting undressed right before we get into it, I say I forgot my purse in the car. I go outside and get my purse, come back in and leave the door unlocked."

"Alright. Make sure you don't leave and get the phone until right before yall fuck." Don instructed.

"Damn does it matter!!" Dana said almost screaming.

"Yeah cause niggas don't think straight when they dick hard. That way he won't get suspicious. We might call your phone while you in there, just act like we one of your girls."

Their conversation was interrupted by a horn blowing outside. All this time Odell was picking her up from Don house and didn't have a clue. Alright baby I'm out of here, Dana said while grabbing her Pelle Pelle leather.

"Come here baby, we gone be there in a couple hours. Make sure you stall out cause we gotta wait on Jake."

"Why yall even need him? It's only one person." Dana asked.

73

"That's my man, plus he bringing the mac, I'm not just gone run in there with this nine. I wanna pump fear in this nigga, so he give that shit right up."

"Beep!! Beep!! (horn blowing) Alright I'm out of here." Dana stated as she walked out the door.

It was about 10:30 pm when Don made it to Rome's house on Mt. Elliott. Rome was standing in front of the house leaning on a beat up Chevy Caprice talking to his moms. The Caprice was a fiend rental Debra had got for him. He claimed he was going to the movies with his girl, but she knew something was up. He had on an all-black jogging suit with some all black Air Force ones, any other time he'd be dress to impress.

"Boy just make sure you be careful. Debra told her son looking him directly in the eye."

"Ma what is you talking bout?" Rome asked playing the stupid role.

"Boy don't forget I birthed you, I know when something going on."

"Ma ain't nothing going on."

"Yeah ok, just remember what I said." Don walked up while Rome was finishing his conversation with his mother.

"Whatup doe? Jake hit you up yet?" He asked instantly.

"Naw."

"Fuck taking this nigga so long." Don was anxious. His palms was itching.

"Be easy dog, it ain't nothing but like 11:00 pm. Dana just left a hour ago right?"

"Yeah." Don responded.

"We cool, be patient."

Chapter 12

Southwest Detroit, the only part of the City that was gang affiliated. It was mostly filled with Mexicans, Blacks, Puerto Ricans, and Caldean families spreaded throughout but for the most part this was Mexican territory. Jake's cousin Omar was born and raised in Southwest. He had an apartment off Fort St. making a little noise. Omar was 19, one of those by any means hustlers. He didn't follow none of the rules or principles of the game, which was common nowadays. In his case though it was extra dangerous because he was young and dumb and didn't understand the consequences. The game ain't fair to nobody, but it really ain't fair to those who burn bridges and shiest for a living. Jake loved visiting Omar and the feeling was mutual. He loved being around the hustle and he looked up to Omar. Omar knowing this, took advantage of him, he'd let him sit in the spot all day rolling. Jake would make Omar a couple thousand, but he would just give him $75 and let him play the Super Nintendo all day. Smoke up some weed and gas his head up about how they gone take shit over and get some real money. Jake even started to bring his own money to the table, Omar would just tax him for the weight. Plus them little quarters and half ounces he was buying weren't enough to see a real profit. He had to cut the rocks too big to keep Omar clientele coming. Eventhough Jake was young, in his heart, he knew he was getting played.

He didn't care though, this was big cuz and he did it out of love, plus he felt like he was being educated.

"Man how many times I gotta tell you stop playing with that," Omar said while snatching the Mac-11 out of Jake's hand.

"I don't know man I'm just in love with that mothafucka, Jake said grinning like a kid in the candy store. Niggas ain't ready for this shit, he said while picking it up off the coffee table. Hey, you need to let me hold this for this lick I got up for tonight?"

"Man sit your ass down, hand me that money, I gottta go holler at my peoples."

"Don't take all day dog, you know I gotta leave in a minute. I got that thing with Rome and them."

"You need to stay here and get this real money, keep robbing them white boys and shit they gone bury yall under the jail."

"Naw this the real deal right here, and I can't let my peoples down." Jake said in defense.

"Whatever I be right back, Omar countered while scooping up the Mac and heading for the door.

"Hold on dog, you taking the Mac with you?"

"Nigga you don't need this, I'm only going around the corner. I left my other burners over Grandma crib. You'll be straight, I'll be right back. Plus niggas know we around here," said Omar overconfident.

"Whatever man" Jake responded.

Omar pulled off in his Monte SS. He told Jake he was meeting his connect, but his real plans was to slide off, get some pussy and leave Jake there to finish off the rest of the work. First he had to run to his Grandma's and grab the 4-5, shoot back to the apartment, drop it off and run back out. He couldn't leave his little cousin in there naked that was a no-no.

Meanwhile Jake was at the apartment, music blasting, smoking a blunt while playing the video game at the same time. Doing exactly what his cousin told him not to do over and over again. Outside, a black conversion van pulled up and parked directly across the street from the apartment. Three man sat in the van with their ski masks rolled up. The driver broke the silence while cocking back the P-89 Ruger in his hand.

"Yeah that's the apartment building right there."

"How we gone get in there though?" the chubby one in the backseat asked.

"Man that shit ain't nothing, he slanging out the apartment. All we gotta do is send a fiend in there and we follow suit right behind. Bitch ass niggas playing the game raw, he gone get what he deserve."

One of Omar's cons was selling people synthetic cocaine, or usually whatever he could put together. These boys fell victim. He sold them 4 ½ ounces of Vitamin A cut and Oragel. Omar figured since they was from Southfield, a suburb of Detroit that they was soft and would go for anything. Uncle Moe had been around for a long time. He started smoking crack when it was an expensive high and it was looked at as cool. He pulled up to Omar's spot with a young tender with him, a runaway 16 year old and Moe had turned her out already. She was smoking like I-75 going north. The driver of the van spotted Moe on his way into the building.

"Hey ol school, can I holla at you for a minute?" he asked.

"Whatsup youngblood."

"Hey look I need a favor, I got a $50 spot for you. I need to get inside this apartment in that building, we just gone follow you in when you knock on the door."

"They don't let nobody in there youngblood, under no circumstances, they serve you through a slot."

"Look man, I got a c-note for you, I know you know how to get in there," the driver said with his face balled up.

Uncle Moe was old school, he'd seen this scene play out many times. He wasn't a big fan of Omar, but he'd knew him his whole life. Plus he noticed his car was gone, which is the main reason why he stopped. He owed Omar some money, so he was trying to hurry up, cop and leave. In his heart, he knew these boys was up to no good, but his greed was outweighing his rationale. He looked at his young tender in the passenger seat and thought about what he could do with the $100.

"Look yall ain't gone kill nobody right? Just a smooth robbery, in and out." Uncle Moe asked not really wanting to know the answer.

"C'mon man, do I look like a killer?"

Uncle Moe looked at him like he had a hole in his head. "Youngblood I been on these streets too long. I done seen it all, then some. You can't run game this way."

With that said Uncle Moe and the three masked man made their way through the entrance. The apartment building was only four stories high, with six rooms on each floor. Most of the tenants were either crackheads or heroin addicts. A few young single parent mothers were spreaded throughout the building. Omar had the whole building in debt to him one way or the other. He took care of their habit all through the month and doubled sometimes tripled their debt when they received their check on the first, third and fifteenth of the month. Soon as they reached the top floor where Omar's apartment was located, music could be heard thumping through the walls. Uncle Moe knocked on the door, well he actually banged cause the music was too loud for Jake to hear a knock.

"Whatsup what you trying to do?" Jake answered.

"Youngblood where Omar at? I got some of that green for him, plus I'm trying to buy two 8-balls."

"Alright, slide it through the slot."

"C'mon youngblood, you know I gotta see mine weighed out on the scale," Uncle Moe pleaded.

"Who that Uncle Moe?"

"Yeah."

"Man as many times as you done been here, you know it's all there, quit playing, I ain't got all day," Jake said feeling bossy. Growing impatient the leader of the three men nudged Uncle Moe in the side with his P-89. Urging him to hurry up before someone appeared in the hallway.

"Who is this youngblood, who was in here last time...., um, what's his name."

"Jake."

"Oh yeah man, let me in, you remember Omar let me clean up and we smoked that good weed." Uncle Moe said, talking so fast it almost sounded like jibberish.

"Man hold up!"

The locks sounded from behind the door at the same time the three men pulled their ski masks down. "Man you acting like you...," before Jake could finish his sentence. The masked men burst in, the first one smacking him upside the head with the butt of the pistol. He was leaking instantly. Uncle Moe ran off down the hall so fast, he probably left a trail of smoke behind him.

"What the fuck!!" Jake muffled out in pain.

"Search the spot real fast. Where the fuck Omar at little nigga?"

"I don't know."

"Wrong answer cuz!" The leader of the three shouted as he smacked Jake upside the head again.

The other two were done searching the apartment and came up empty handed. Besides the $1,200 and change Jake had in his pockets, they was assed out. Omar was smart enough to not leave anything in the apartment, plus he rarely let Jake hold any real cash.

"Wasn't shit in there dog," the other two men came back telling the driver.

"Man yall playing with fire, soon as cuz find out about this shit, yall done." Jake shouted showing he had heart.

"Oh yeah, make sure you tell Omar he fucked with the wrong ones, and to take this with him, BLOC!! BLOC!! BLOC!!" was the last sounds Jake would ever hear.

Chapter 13

"Damn why you keep pacing around like you ain't never been over here before or something. You on some other shit. I don't know though, keep on pacing cause that ass is looking kind of fat nowadays." Odell said with a devious grin.

Dana kept walking around the house, picking up things and putting them back down, opening the refrigerator door and closing it. Her nervous antics were obvious, Ray Charles could of seen something wasn't right. In her own little way Dana wanted Odell to peep that something wasn't right, her conscious was kicking in, but it was no way she could lie to Don or back out without hearing his mouth. Odell would have to realize it on his own and make the operation go stale. The nigga was on cloud nine though, the cognac mixed with the three el's he smoked, had his mind on one thing, pussy, pussy, pussy.

"Baby come here, " Odell said while rubbing his dick. Dana walked over to him and stood in between his legs as he sat on the couch. "Sit down why you standing there looking stupid?"

The sounds of the muffler and the tires hitting the pavement was all you heard as Rome and Don headed to Odell's house. Inside the car, it was so quiet you could hear a pin drop. Any other time there would be some music blasting to get they mind right or a bunch of commotion back and forth. No words were exchanged, both of them knew what each other were thinking. It didn't feel right without their other half. Something wasn't right, Jake wouldn't just not show up, not how he was pressing them or as excited as he was. This was what he lived for, it didn't add up.

"Man, I can't believe this nigga stood us up," Don broke the silence. "He probably somewhere high out his mind fucking with Omar."

"Fuck it, it's too late for all that now, we a worry about that later." Rome spoke up irritated. "We sticking to the script, same routine ain't nothing changed since he ain't here. Dude soft, he gone give that shit up."

Don nodded his head looking at Rome while he was driving. Little did Rome know that's exactly what he needed to hear. The whole time they were riding he was tapping his fingers against his kneecaps while flicking the safety on and off on the nine. Those words from Rome calmed his nerves and boosted his confidence.

"Yeah you right dog, let's get this bread, it's about time we got our cash up." Don responded.

They pulled up around the corner from Odell's house right off Morang Ave. Turned the car off, got out and left the keys in the ignition. With them being shorthanded, that was a must, anything can happen, there was no time to be unlocking doors and fiddling with keys. From what they scoped out earlier and to their advantage, it was a bus stop in front of the house next door to Odell's. Don and Rome posted up like they were waiting on the bus to kill the suspicion. As soon as Dana came to the driveway to get her purse out of the car, she would go back in with the door unlocked, and they would rush in behind. It was flaws in the setup, but that's in any plan. The neighborhood was nice, but it

84

wasn't upscale. It was about 1:30 am and most of the neighbors were sleep. This worked to Don and Rome's advantage because little did they know, the bus stop running an hour ago. So actually standing at the bus stop at 1 in the morning, they stuck out like a sore thumb and it was obvious they were up to something. Rookie mistakes.

"Damn man, what the fuck is up with Jake, now we gotta go in here with these punk as pistols." Don spoke up while he positioned the nine in his waistband, as they waited patiently. Rome had a 38 special and he had the high-point. It wasn't the Mac-11 Don was missing, Jake was the muscle, intimidator, his aggression gave them confidence.

"Shit man you still stuck on that, we just gone have to get the job done with these. Worry about your girl, she the one taking her time."

"Speaking of the devil, here she come right now."

Damn I hope this niggas have this money right, he bet not of fell asleep without finishing that work. These were the only thoughts that crossed Omar's mind as he was pulling up to the apartment building right off of Fort St. What he saw when he pulled up almost made him drop his blunt out his hand. Squad cars were everywhere, the coroner van was parked on the grass near the entrance.

"Fuck!! Please don't tell me they coming out of my apartment. Please, fuck no!" Omar said to himself.

You know the saying, "hope for the best, prepare for the worse." Well I doubt if he expected or was prepared for this one. Three men exited with a bodybag loading it into the van. Omar stood there shell shocked watching from afar at the other end of the block.

"Omar, Omar, where you been boy? Everybody been looking for you, somebody ran in your spot and killed that little young nigga you be with. They robbed him to." Nessa, a young girl who was about 16 from around the corner told him. She was so excited to have some information for him, she sounded like the chipmunks she was talking so fast. Nessa was still rambling on and on, but Omar was off in space. He didn't hear a word she was saying, everything after they killed that young nigga you be with was a blur. "You taking the Mac with you," were the words that kept replaying in his head over and over. Guilt overwhelmed him, not only did he leave his cousin in there naked, but while he was somewhere fucking one of his duckheads, Jake was getting his brains blew out. In most cases, everytime you break one of the commandments of the game, you gotta pay for it. If you don't pay for it, someone close to you will, no one is immune to becoming a casualty. Omar knew what he had to do, send a message, make an example. This was like a spit in the face. He burned so many bridges, he didn't know where to turn first, but he know he'd get to the bottom of it. When he came to his senses, Nessa was still talking.

"Man ain't nobody see nothing?" Omar asked.

"Boy did you hear anything I just said?" Nessa stood there in her bowlegged stance with her hands on her hips smacking her teeth. She had a crush on Omar, so she would run the story down over and over just for an excuse to be in his presence. "Tonya on the third floor say she seen Uncle Moe talking to somebody outside not too long before it happened."

"Man Uncle Moe ain't doing nothing like that, he praise the ground I walk on, plus he know how I'm cut. Arrogance can be a weakness, which Omar failed to realize. Even at this point, he was still hard headed.

"Baby hold up," Odell said stopping Dana from kissing on his neck. "I got something for you, go outside and get that bag from out the backseat of my truck."

"Why Odell, is it that serious?"

"Yeah, I want you to put on something. Fuck it, I'll go get it," Odell said trying to stand up.

Dana pushed him down instantly. "Chill don't worry, I got it, give me the keys. This nigga just don't know, he making it easier than I thought and I didn't even wanna do this shit. I hope these niggas outside," Dana thought to herself.

Odell was digging a hole for himself. Dana mind was so dis-combobulated she didn't leave her purse in the truck as planned,. Odell had just sealed his fate without knowing.

"Alright cuz, soon as she make it back to the door, we gone snatch her up." Rome stated.

"I know the drill."

"There them fools go right there, they look like they up to something. It's kind of nippy out here too, that's just a sign something about to go down." Dana was mumbling under her breath as she made her way to Odell's truck. She grabbed the Victoria Secret bag out the truck and made her way to the steps. Rome snatched her up before her hand reached the doorknob.

"Open the door up bitch!!" Rome said as he gripped her by the throat and put the 38 to her head.

"Damn nigga you playing the role a little too hard ain't you?" Dana snapped

"Shut the fuck up and follow my lead." (screaming) Ahhhhh!! Ahhhhh!!! Ahhhhh!!!

Rome throws Dana into the floor. She hit the ground yelling as if she was having a baby. Odell sat there on his couch in his boxers with his mouth open. He looked at the two men before him, even with their shades and fitted caps on, he could tell they were young. At one point everything seemed to move in slow motion the ceiling fan went from high to low, and the slow jams started to sound screwed up in the background.

"Bitch get yo ass up!" Rome snatched Dana off the ground. He had the 38 special jammed in her neck.

"You know what it is nigga, cooperate, show us where the bread at before we blow this bitch head off." Don cocked the nine aiming it at Odell.

"Aha ha ha ha!!" To everyone surprise, Odell just burst out laughing. "Man I don't give a fuck what you do to that bitch. It's part of the game, it is what it is." Dana was crushed, she tried to hold it in, but to no avail, a single tear rolled down her face. Odell cockiness threw everyone off.

"Look man, I don't know what yall talking bout anyways, ain't nothing in here besides what you see, take what you want." Odell had been a stick-up kid before he jumped in the dope game. He sensed they were amateurs, in his heart he felt he could take them. He just had to regain the upper hand. "These niggas is scared," he thought, but he also knew a scared man would kill.

"Oh you think it's a game huh, get yo silly ass on the floor belly first, put your hands behind your back. Hey dog, hand me them cuffs." Rome handed Don the handcuffs out of his back pocket. A million thoughts were running through Odell's head. He wasn't about to let these young dudes handcuff him. His ego was kicking in, and he wasn't going out like this, especially not in front of his girl. He had to make a move and make it fast.

Omar sat in front of Jake's home on his third pint of Remy V.S. while smoking his 2nd blunt. He had been sitting in front for at least an hour trying to build up the strength to tell his Aunt Renee the news. He thought he lost his conscious years ago, but the way it was eating at him now, proved otherwise. Omar looked up at the house and saw one of the bedroom lights on. It was obvious she had company, which was usually the only time she was home. No one wanted to bear the news to a single mother that she lost her only son. Emilio Sparks said it best, ["I mean what do you say to a woman who just lost her only son to the game and the gunning"]. He wanted to just pull off, but he figured it was the least he could do because he held himself responsible. Omar knocked on the door for a good ten minutes, before Renee answered the door breathing heavily with disheveled hair wearing a negligee.

"Omar? Boy I ain't seen you in God knows when, Jake not here, what you doing beating on my door this late?"

"Aunt Renee can I come in for a minute? I need to talk to you about something."

"About what? Plus I got company and you interrupting. Hurry up."

"Alright." Omar said while he tried to step inside the house. He was stopped in his tracks.

"Uh huh. You can talk to me from right here." Omar just shook his head.

"You sure?"

"Positive."

"Auntie, Jake dead."

"What!! What you mean Jake dead? Not my son Jake. What the fuck happened!" Her reaction shocked Omar, it was more anger than sadness. That's just natural instinct, at first it takes awhile to set in.

"You had him over there in that apartment, didn't you? I told that boy about hanging over there with your scurvy ass."

Omar approached her to try to hug her, but she pushed him away, and started to beat on his chest.

"Get the fuck away from me! Where the fuck were you? Why they ain't kill your ass? Get the fuck away from me Omar, and where you think you going?"

"Huh?" The male voice answered who was visiting Renee. "I figured you wanted some privacy after what you just heard."

"Get your ass back upstairs in that bed nigga. I ain't done with you yet." Omar couldn't believe his ears, he just told her, her son was killed and she still had dick on the brain.

"And you gone pay for the fucking funeral too! Have my money ready tomorrow." Renee shouted as she shut the door in his face.

****

Don was trying to put the cuffs on Odell while holding the pistol at the same time. He was so anxious, he wasn't concentrating on what he was doing. Suddenly a car alarm went off outside. This startled Rome and he took his eyes off Odell for a quick second. Bad move. Odell kicked his feet up under the glass table shattering it. Glass flew in Don's face and he was momentarily stunned. The gun slid across the floor as Odell dove towards Rome. They tussled for what seemed like eternity until two shots sealed Odell's fate.

Rome: "Hey man I told you not to make this shit incriminating."

Rio: "What the fuck are you talking about?"

Rome: "Dog, read between the lines, you know what I'm saying don't play the dumb role. I don't know why I let you talk me into this. I'm going against everything I love right now. This shit too close to dry snitching. Jake probably turning over in his grave."

91

Rio: "Look man, you felt like yall story was worth telling. One minute you loving the limelight, next you hiding from the cameras."

Rome: "That's how I was raised, they say a picture worth a thousand words. Indictments don't have no time limitations. This ain't a game and it never was."

Rio: "Man c'mon with the bullshit, you over doing it."

Rome: "You can never be overdoing it."

Rio: "Dog, man the fuck up!! It's too late in the game for all that."

Rome: "Hold on boss, I don't know who you think you talking too. I think you been reading and writing too many of these hood novels. Check your tone."

Rio: "Alright tough guy, I'm moving along with the story."

Dana was quiet as a church mouse as she lowered the pistol. Her palms were sweaty and she was shaking like a leaf.

"Fuck!! Fuck!! Fuck!! Now we ain't gone be able to get shit off him!" Don said while jumping around stomping his feet and throwing a tantrum. He threw his fitted on the floor and put his face in his palms. Don and Rome proceeded to search the house frantically, but not thoroughly. The shooting had them thrown off mentally.

"Fuck it man, we gotta get out of here, I know somebody heard them shots." Rome said as he was searching the closet in the bedroom. "We out!"

"Fuck that, we not leaving here without nothing dog. Grab that nigga keys, we can take his truck to Chuck's shop."

"Man you tripping, I ain't trying to hear that."

Don ran out the house bare faced and hopped in the truck. He sat there for a minute as if he was waiting for Rome and Dana to get in. Dana looked on from the porch, Rome was already halfway across the street.

"C'mon Dana, what the fuck? Dana! Dana!" Rome shouted.

Dana just stood there as if she was in the twilight zone. Eyes bulging, looking like a manican. Rome ran back and snatched her off the porch, she almost fell on her face. Don had already pulled out the driveway and was halfway up the block. Meanwhile Rome had to basically drag Dana to the beat up Chevy. She was two-stepping like she had all the time in the world. "I should of left this bitch on the porch, " is what crossed Rome mind as he started up the hooptie.

Chapter 14

Whens the last time you heard a funeral home going out of business? Just about never, especially in an urban area. Swanson funeral home on Grand Blvd. and Mack Ave. wasn't an exception. Very few attended the memorial being held at this moment. Only eight or nine people were at the service for Jason Moore aka Jake. The Reverend shook his head at the podium as he thought about another adolescent gone before his time. At the tender age of 16, Jake had barely gotten a chance to live his life. The people at the service seemed like they were there more out of necessity then genuine concern. They stood around like they couldn't wait for the service to be over. Renee arranged the funeral just three days after he was pronounced dead. Some members of the family didn't even know. Renee neglected her son so much, she barely knew who to contact about his death.

"Auntie, did you tell his boys, um, Donnie and Rome about Jake?" Omar asked leaning down whispering in Renee's ear.

"Donnie and who?"

"Don and Rome, his friends Auntie!"

"Oh, I rode around looking for them boys, I don't know where they live, shit."

With that said Omar stormed out of the funeral home.

You ever heard a drug addict speak on experiencing their first high? Whether its heroin, cocaine, marijuana or ecstasy, doesn't matter everyone

94

remembers there first time. The when, where, how and why will forever be etched in there memory. More importantly, the feeling they got, whether it was a downer or upper, eased the pain or increased it. Now you're not addicted to the drug, but the chase. You're chasing that first high you'll never experience again, unbeknownst to you. The game is just like any other drug. One taste and it can suck you in. With a murder, robbery gone wrong, Dana, Don and Rome was high off the rush and didn't even realize it. This was the breaking point, everything else they did in the past was child's play. At ages 15 and 16, they'd just experienced their first taste.

Rome sat in his room waiting on Don to pull up so they could take Odell's truck to Chuck's Chop Shop. Stealing cars wasn't their thing, but they figured they could at least get 3 or 4 grand for the truck at the least. Rome had just hung up the phone with Don. He was paranoid, not only because of the incident, but Dana hadn't spoken a single word since she pulled the trigger.

"Dana, Dana! Dana talk to me baby, you scaring me." Don yelled while shaking her shoulders. Dana sat huddled in the corner with her knees to her chest. The same spot she'd been in since the night they got back. Every now and then she would hum and rock back and forth. She hadn't washed in days and was starting to smell. If anyone ever doubted Don's love for Dana, that was history, because the average nigga would of left her somewhere. Dana was traumatized, committing the murder, along with everything else she witnessed in life broke her down mentally. Being abused as a child, no mother, no father and an over-protective grandmother who felt she was inferior.

"Dana baby, I'm going to see Rome, I be back in a minute alright. C'mon Dana you stronger than that, say something to me baby."

"Hmmm Hmmm Hmmm," She continued to hum.

"Huh? Baby I be back." Dana needed to get her act together. Don's mother was starting to get suspicious.

"Boy what's wrong with that child?"

"Nothing Ma, she just not feeling well," Don said as he left the house.

"Man I don't know what the fuck is up with Dana, she got me on edge." Don stated as soon as he got to Rome's house.

"I know man, I think that shit fucked her head up."

"What we gone do?" Don asked.

"What you mean, what we gone do? Nigga that's your girl."

"Oh, so it's like that?"

"Nah, I'm just playing, she'll come around sooner or later. Let's hurry up and get to Chuck's shop. Get rid of this hot ass truck."

****

Omar bent the corner just as Don and Rome were pulling off. Omar remembered the house he used to drop Jake off to, but he never went inside. He sat in front of Rome's house and blew the horn a couple times, but no one came to the door. Just as he was about to pull off, Dave the bum who you could find in front of the store whether it was open or closed, rain, sleet, hail or snow was approaching the house.

"Hey my man, can you deliver a message for me?"

"To who, and who is it from?" Dave said in a tone indicating he didn't wanna be bothered.

"I don't know you," Dave lied he knew practically every car that passed by the area more than twice, shit he lived outside.

"Here man." Omar said handing a twenty dollar bill through the window. "Tell the little niggas who live here that Jake got killed, his funeral going on right now. Can you do that?"

"That ain't something you wanna deliver personally?"

"Look man, time is money." Omar said as he pulled off.

Chuck's Auto Body Shop was located on French Rd and Gratiot. If you walked in there you would see the same parts sitting around collecting dust. Inventory was almost non-existent. The body shop was a front for a larger operation. If you was good people and had cash on hand, the sky was the limit as to what you could get your hands on. The shop looked just like any other shabby ran down building on the block. Chuck came out of the shop wearing his usual attire. Oil stained dickies and steel toe boots. This, adding to the fact that he rode

97

around in a Sanford and Son pickup truck everyday, you'd never guess he was a self-made millionaire. Chuck was old school, he knew the streets was watching, but more importantly the alphabet boys. It's not about how much money you make, longevity is the key, he not only understood that, he lived it. Rome knew Chuck because he was an old friend of his mothers. They use to run together back in the day when Debra was a flight attendant. Chuck was in the game heavy back then, and well, you know the rest, one hand washed the other.

"Boy I know you ain't got into stealing cars?" Chuck said more as a statement than asking a question.

"C'mon Chuck, you know that ain't my style."

"Shit you young niggas don't believe in style anymore. Yall don't have no finesse or nothing. Jump off the porch with a blind fold on, bringing unnecessary heat on the real ones."

Rome wasn't trying to hear no lecture, but he knew it was a given when he was in the presence of Chuck. Plus he needed him right now, so he had to feed his ego.

"Yeah, you right Chuck." Rome said cutting him off.

"You don't have to tell me, I know I'm right. How your moms and grandma doing?"

"Good."

"Tell them I be by there to check up on them, I gotta take them these pictures of the kids too. So whatsup, what you need?"

"Chuck how much can you give me for this truck?"

"I don't know what you talking bout."

"Huh?"

Rome stood there dumbfounded as Chuck motioned for him to step outside the shop. To this day, Chuck stay paranoid. He barely talked indoors, especially at the shop.

"Always watch what you say indoors, and who is that in the passenger seat?" Chuck asked referring to Don, who sat in the truck bobbing his head to the radio.

"Oh that's my man Don, he cool."

"Ain't nobody cool in this game son. Pull the truck inside the shop and tell your boy to wait outside."

Rome walked to the truck and informed Don to wait while he pulled the truck inside, he noticed Don was wearing the same hat he wore the night of the robbery.

"Damn dog you got on the same hat you wore that night, whatsup with you, you slipping."

"This not the same one stupid, this brand new."

"Still dog, you shouldn't even be wearing that shit. I be right back."

Rome pulled into the shop as Chuck and two of his employees stood waiting. Chuck's employees went right to work on the 98' Tahoe.

"Step into my office Rome." Chuck signaled Rome outside in the backyard of the shop. "Here." He says as he hands Rome an envelope. "That's 4 grand."

"Damn that's all," Rome says irritated. "The keys still in it and everything."

"Look man, I don't even deal with this shit no more, I'm only doing it cause it's you." Chuck stated, running the same game he ran on everybody. You know how it goes, the ones who got the money is always the tightest. That's probably the reason why they got it.

"Hey Chuck come here right quick!" One of his workers called from the inside.

"Hold on!"

"Naw you need to see this."

Chuck and Rome stepped back inside to see most of the Tahoe stripped down. To their amazement, the worker held a block of cocaine wrapped in an oven bag in his hand.

"What he had a stash box?" Chuck asked.

"Yep, right under the gas tank."

Rome eyes lit up like a Christmas tree, Don ain't gone believe this, he thought.

"What you gone do?" Chuck snaps Rome out of his daze.

"Huh?"

"You want me to have somebody get rid of it for you?"

"Naw, I'm cool, I got it."

Chuck motioned Rome and stepped back outside. "Boy that's probably a little over a half a bird in there, what you gone do with that type of weight?"

"I got it Chuck, I can handle it." Chuck just smirked and shook his head.

"Listen to me Rome, look at me while I'm talking. The game ain't what it seem to be. It's always two sides to every story. You gotta make your mind up early, you either gone be ten toes in this shit or you ain't. Understand?"

Rome nodded, but the words were going in one ear and out the other. Later on in life, he would understand exactly what Chuck was telling him though.

Chapter 15

"Why the fuck these people keep driving off and pulling back up in front of the house. I know they not looking this way, this boy bet not of done nothing crazy." Don's mother Regina spoke under her breath while looking outside her blinds. Little did she know her suggestions were true. Her house was the target, but they weren't looking for her son, the culprit was sitting in his room in the same spot she'd been in for days. Outside was the missing persons unit of the D.P.D. In fact, Dana's grandmother had exaggerated Dana's disappearance so much, the local police had called in help from the Feds.

"Hell fuck yeah, see nigga, and you ain't even wanna take the truck. See how shit turn around." Don said rubbing his hands together bouncing up and down in the backseat of the cab. He was elated. "We on now, you said it's a half a chirp right?"

"Yeah I think that's what Chuck was saying. He asked me did I want him to get rid of it."

"So, what you gone do?"

"I'm a take it to the crib and try to catch Ski or one of them and see what the numbers is on this shit right now."

The cab came to a stop in front of Rome's house. Don stopped him as he was about to pay for the cab. Don informed him that he would pay because he was going to his house to check on his mother and Dana. "I be right back, look, don't do nothing without me."

"Man calm down, I'll be here when you get back." As soon as Rome entered the house Debra was on his heels.

"Boy where you been? Some boy named Omar dropped a message off for you."

Rome ignored his mother and continued up the steps toward his room "Jerome D'andre Wilson!!" He knew his mother meant business whenever she called his full name, but he was in a rush to stash the cocaine.

No sooner than he sat on his bed, his mother burst through the door. "Boy I know you heard me calling you..." Her words were cut short as she was stunned to see her son sitting on the bed with an oven bag full of cocaine.

"Oh so you wanna be a drug dealer now huh?"

"Ma how you just gone burst in my room like that?"

"Shutup you don't pay no bills here, I do what I wanna do. Your friend Jake got killed, his funeral was yesterday.

"What! How you know?"

"Some boy named Omar left a message with Dave that be on the corner."

Rome dropped his head, but was too upset to shed a tear at the moment.

"You gone be ok?"

Rome nodded.

"Alright come downstairs when you get yourself together, we need to talk."

"Alright, it's time we move on to the premises, we have another anonymous tip that this young lady frequents this home. Did you get the warrant?" The officers sat outside Don's home communicating through their walkie talkies. "Alright move in." Just as Don's cab was pulling up, he saw two men in suits walking toward his front door. His first mind was to tell the driver to keep going, but curiosity and cockiness led him to get out anyway.

"Excuse me young man, you live here?"

"Why what's going on?"

"You not in any trouble or anything, we just wanna know if you seen or know this young lady?" The officer showed him a picture of Dana.

"No sir."

"Well we have reason to believe she's been staying at this home. Mind if we take a look around, we have a warrant."

Don wasn't expecting that, and his expression gave him away. He was nervous Pervis as they opened the door. In the inside he was praying Dana had left. Went for a walk, to the mall, or something, anything but here. He knew the chances were slim to none, considering the condition she'd been in the last few days. Don's mother wasn't home, so that was a good sign.

"Don't look like anyone here." Don said digging himself a bigger hole.

"We'll only be a few, " the plain suits stated as they looked around room to room. They heard a sneeze and went straight to Don's room.

"Ahhh!! What the hell!!" Dana quickly covered herself as she just gotten out the shower. A smile crept across Don's face by hearing her reaction he realized she had came to her senses. The plain suit officer quickly shut the door and started talking through the crack.

"Dana were gonna need you to get dressed and step out the bedroom, were from the D.P.D. missing persons unit and there has been a report put out on you by your grandmother Violetta Wiles."

"Man she get on my nerves, she knew where I was, so what yall gone do?"

"She's still your legal guardian under law, we have to return you to her residence." Dana stepped out the room looking far from an adolescent. The detectives tried to maintain there gawking, but to no avail. Don broke the awkwardness.

"So, what yall gone do?" Yall stay in here too long niggas gone think I'm snitching."

"Oh we gone be on our way, and we gotta take you down for questioning, to make sure Dana wasn't taken against her will."

"That's not necessary, that's my boyfriend." Dana cut in.

"Well we showed him a photo of you before we came in and he claim he didn't know you. If he would have just told the truth from the jump, we wouldn't have this problem. Now we have to look into it. Johnson cuff him up and get him down to the station. Now you really don't have to worry about looking like a snitch. Dana follow me."

"Baby call me as soon as you get down there, they on some bullshit. I know what to do, I got you!" Dana yelled back as they were being led in opposite direction.

That's the way the game go, you win some, you lose some. These were terms Rome could never agree with. He wanted his cake and to eat it too, he wanted to be the exception. When you look at it, when it comes to the game that's what everyone is chasing. Everybody wants to be the exception to the rule. Doesn't matter how many you witness before you die or go to prison. You're special, it won't happen to you. Naw, you too smart for that, you gone learn from they mistakes. You and your team gone be the exception, the success story. Yeah it's been success stories in the past, but what did they have to sacrifice and what's the ratio? You fail to look at the odds. You're blinded by your addiction, before you realize it, it impairs your judgment. Either one or two things happen when the game puts you through something you've never experienced. You either get all the way out or go all the way in harder. At 16, Rome was oblivious to the importance of how his decisions would affect him.

Rome made his way down the steps after a hour and a half. He was hoping his mother was gone, but she sat at the kitchen table smoking a cigarette.

106

"You alright?" she asked.

"Yeah Ma, why you keep asking me that?"

"Boy stop trying to act tough, I had you remember?"

"For real Ma, it seem like everytime I look up somebody gone, I done ran out of tears, plus that shit ain't gone do me no good. I gotta ride for the cause, that's how Jake would of wanted it."

"Listen to you, you sound real stupid right now. Ain't nothing you can do about that shit, leave it alone and learn from it."

"Ma who you think you talking too!!" Rome says as he hops out of his chair and starts to pace.

"Boy sit your ass down, I'm still your mother."

"Naw I ain't mean it like that, but c'mon stop treating me like I don't know what's going on. You think I'm blind or something, everybody talking it, but not walking it. Real live hypocrites! We not better than nobody down the street or around the corner. The slums affecting us like everybody else. I know you want more for me, but I'm tired, I'm tired man. Tired of barely making it, when the recipe on how to make it is right in front of me."

"Oh so you think that's the recipe, boy you just don't know…"

"C'mon ma, practice what you preach," Rome cut her off.

" No, damn, listen for a minute, that's your problem." Sniff, sniff, "Debra started sniffling and her eyes started to water. Look I know I haven't been the best mother, and I have may faults, but it's gone get better, baby I promise. I know I gotta get me together, and I'm working on that. Everything that glitters ain't gold Jerome. Trust me whatever you after is a want, not a need. You may not have the best, but you got everything you need. Focus on getting your ass up out of here and going to school. You hear me?" Debra looked into her sons eyes and noticed at that instant, everything she said fell on deaf ears. It was a slight pause and silence between them.

"So, Ma you gone help me get rid of this work?" I got 500 grams of soft?"

"Oh my God, I done created a monster," Debra thought to herself.

Chapter 16

3600 Beaubien, the Detroit Police Det. Headquarters downtown. Trust me, you didn't wanna be here unless you were playing or coaching in a basketball game for P.A.L. League (Police Athletic League) anything else meant bad news. Don sat in a dimly lit room handcuffed to a chair, on the opposite side of the table sat Det. Barnes. He had an arrogant look on his face as he played with the toothpick between his lips. All you could hear was the sound of him tapping his fingers against the table, or Don fidgeting around every five seconds.

"This gone be easy," Detective Barnes thought as a smirk appeared on his face. You know why you here right?"

"Man like I told the last one that was in here, that's my girlfriend, she even told yall that. Ain't nobody kidnap her, her grandma playing games cause she don't like me."

"Ah ha ha ha, ha ha" (laughter) Detective Barnes let out a slight chuckle. Don didn't find shit funny. Barnes noticed the confused look on his face.

"They didn't tell you huh? That's what you think this is about, oh I could care less about you and your little hoodrat. Naw, you dealing with the big boys now."

"Man what the fuck is you talking bout?"

"This is what I'm talking bout, right here," Barnes raises his voice and slams 3 photos of Odell's body sprawled across his floor with his head wide open.

The pictures alone shook Don up. His body language said it all. "Now do you know what I'm talking bout!! Damn tough guy, what happened, speak up."

"What, am I supposed to know him or something?"

"Oh, ok I see, see I was gone try to give you a chance to fess up."

"Fess up to what!" Don tried to stand up, but ended up stumbling.

"Listen little nigga I'm a give you one chance to tell me your side of the story or what you know. If it make a little bit of sense, I might let your case stay in juvenile court to cut you some slack, so your ass won't get natural life. Now you got thirty seconds to start telling me something!"

"I don't have nothing to tell."

"Alright, so tell me why we matched your prints with the ones found in the house. Oh yeah I almost forgot, Barnes stood up and whistled outside the door. Murdock bring that in, damn how could I forget, remember this?"

Don heart dropped as he saw the other detective walk in with a Detroit fitted baseball cap in an evidence bag.

"Now I'll bet my last dollar that this hat fits you perfectly, what you think Murdock?" The other detective nodded his head. Detective Barnes took the cap out the evidence bag, and placed it on Don's head. "Look at that, I'll be damned. Oh wait hold on," Barnes walked up and cocked the fitted on Don's head being arrogant. "That's how you young boys wear it now right? You change your mind yet?"

"Man let me have my phone call."

Rome: "Damn man it's always the fluke shit that get a nigga knocked. I swear to this day, I wanna kill Ms. Wiles for reporting Dana missing."

Rio: "Man at the end of the day, it was yall fault."

Rome: "Dog, why is you always cutting me off?"

Rio: "Look who's talking, you just made yourself a part of the book."

Rome: "At this point a saying comes to mind that made a lot of sense to me, "How a nigga start with a ending – way before his beginning." Yeah I can relate. In a sense I think losing the ones closest to me prepared me for what was to come. Instead of fear, it instilled hate and anger. With no direction, but to follow the same motto me and my niggas believed in, get your cash up, I can hear Jake saying it now, get your cash up Rome. (ha ha) (Rome laughs) Damn, I love that nigga. They took my man before his time.

Rio: "I know man, (sniffling) (Rio begins to sob) that shit sad."

Rome: "What, you crying nigga!"

Rio: "Ain't nothing wrong with a grown man crying.'

111

Rome: "Man you ain't even know Jake! This clown............................."

Chapter 17

3 years later (2001)

"What's the deal playboy? My bad dog, I know it's been a minute. I guess once you jump in the fast lane, it's hard to get back over. That's how I been feeling, like everybody else in a traffic jam and I couldn't slow down, if I wanted too. Feel me? Yeah you probably on the tip like, man up nigga. Yeah alright, (Rome smiles) you play that tough role, but we used to have some deep heart to heart talks my guy. But yeah, like I was saying. "Rome pauses to light his blunt, then exhales." I went to visit Don the other day, can you believe it's been 3 years already? That nigga cut up like a bag of dope now too. He claim he not gone drink or smoke when he get out, but I gotta see it to believe it. Um hmmm hmmm (laughter) (Rome giggles) Remember what Pac said, ("He's a changed man, he hit the pen and now no sinning is the game plan.") But you know all this time, I had ol girl taking that weed up there he was playing it like he was smoking, but he was selling that shit. He damn near did a 180 dog, got business plans and all that. He still hounding Dana though, but she running wild. Standup dude though, the average nigga would of gave her up as soon as she jumped ship. They just transferred him from Lapeer up to Ryan, four more left and its downhill from here. I can't wait my nigga real talk. They could of gave my nigga life, but we had one of the best and Silbeck got him a good plea. Shit me, I'm just holding down the fort dog. Trying to get over the hump you know, keep bouncing from a half to a whole slab then back to a half. Shit bout to get better though, I'm looking into some spots on the Westside. My man Dre gone plug me in. Remember him, Bebe's son, you probably don't, you

113

ain't pay niggas no mind." (phone rings) (Rome drops his blunt and steps on it to put it out as he checks his caller ID.) "Well I gotta get out of here my nigga, money calling. Oh yeah, I copped you a new headstone too, you know we gotta stay upgrading," Rome said as he bent down and brushed the dirt off Jake's tombstone.

Rome made it a priority to make it to Elmwood cemetery on Mt. Elliot & Vernor to talk to his mans. Sometimes he would sit at his gravesite and talk for hours. If the average person knew this they'd think he was crazy, but this was mental telepathy for Rome, gave him a piece of mind. He wasn't a big smoker, but he always brought a blunt of the finest weed because he knew Jake loved to smoke. It had been 3 ½ years since Jake was killed and he would have been 19 today. His murder was an unsolved mystery. This really took a toll on the ones who loved him. The only thing that's worse than losing someone is not knowing the perpetrator. Rome still spinned the block on Fort St. and watched the apartment like it just happened yesterday. This was his usual routine after visiting Jake's gravesite.

Omar still had the apartment building doing numbers, but he'd stepped his game up. People in the hood called it the baby carter. He bought the building and sectioned eight every apartment, lease requirements were that you had to keep your mouth shut and have a drug habit, literally. The perks were you could live rent-free, but you had no privacy, any given day or night, Omar or one of his workers would walk in to retrieve product. Or just setup shop and put you out, a notice, forget about it. The old-school Monte SS T-top was a memory. You wouldn't catch him in that nowadays. Naw, he let his workers cop and crash them. Now he matched the whips with the year. If it wasn't a 2000, he

114

wasn't behind the wheel. Omar sat in the driver seat of his bone white Escalade down the street from the building watching the traffic like a crossing guard.

"So, Omar what time is you coming home?' Nessa asked Omar while leaning on the passenger side of his truck with her elbows resting inside the window.

"How many times I gotta tell you that's not my home!! Damn, and stop questioning me."

"Oh, so now it's not your home, I live there, your two kid's bout to be three live there, now it's not your home!! Nessa snapped. Like most childhood crushes, hers turned sour. One on the way and two kids later, she felt like she wasted time with Omar. It was a thin line between love and hate. One minute she loved him, the next she hated his ass.

"I hate you!"

"Nessa I don't give a fuck, get out of my face.'

No sooner than Omar finished his sentence, a 2000 cranberry S-type Jaguar pulled up and parked right behind his Escalade unbeknownst to Nessa. A petite light skinned female got out the driver side with a confident strut. If this was a movie, she could be a double for Rihanna. One look and you could tell she didn't shop at Rainbow. Her toenails and fingernails were done and matched to a tee. The spaghetti strap heels she wore made her ass poke out of her Azzure capris.

"Here baby, Lou's was closed, so I went to the Bread Basket," the young lady says as she kisses Omar on the cheek and hands him his food.

115

"Good looking out baby."

Nessa stood opposite on the passenger side with her mouth open in shock. "Bitch don't you see me standing here!"

The young lady continued talking to Omar as if Nessa was invisible. "Baby I'm a be waiting in the car."

"Naw get in, I want you to take a quick ride with me."

She hesitated for a minute, but proceeded to walk around the truck to the passenger side, knowing damn well she had to get through Nessa to get in the truck. Soon as she reached the passenger door, Nessa surprised her and took a step back clearing her pathway, but not before whispering under her breath.

"Who the fuck wear spaghetti strap heels with capris, tacky bitch."

"Smack! Nessa was blindsided, the young lady backhanded Nessa like she was a pimp and Nessa owed her money. "My mother didn't raise no bitch! I let you slide once...." She said as Nessa stumbled and had to catch her balance. Ohhs and Ahhs could be heard from bystanders on the block. Nessa recovered with an unexpected left hook. It was sloppy, but it caught her right under her chin. That's when all hell broke loose, a cat fight. Omar's lady friend was doing a lot of hair grabbing, Nessa was getting the best of her. He sat in the truck smirking as the fight boosted his ego.

"I don't hear you saying nothing now bitch!" Nessa screamed as she wailed on her. Omar got out the truck to break it up before it got too ugly, he peeped Nessa's friends making their way up the block.

"Nessa get the fuck off of her, what is you doing?" Omar stated like he really cared.

"Get the hell off of me Omar," Nessa was kicking her feet trying to break his hold. "Bitch get up, get up bitch," she said as she tried to spit on her.

"Tory hold Nessa," Omar told one of his workers. He went to help his lady friend up off the ground. "C'mon baby."

"Get the hell off me Omar!! You sat in there and watched that shit!! Trust me, I be back though."

"Bitch you still talking." Nessa was still trying to break loose. She made sure she said bitch everytime she spoke to her.

"I got something for all yall raggedy hoes," she said as she sped off almost crashing her S-type. Rome sat down the street in a rental watching the whole scene unfold, he had his eyes on Omar.

****

["I don't want no scrub, a scrub is a guy that can't get no love from me, sitting in the passenger side of his best friends ride, trying to holler at me."] Dana sang along to her theme music as she got dressed. She smacked her lips as she noticed the letter from Don on her dresser that she still hadn't opened. It had been sitting in the same spot since her grandma dropped it off. She moved out 1 year and a half ago, which is the last time she wrote Don. She felt like it was nothing else to

117

talk about after 3 ½ years. "Let me see what this nigga want," she said to herself as she opened the letter.

Dana,

Whatsup ma? Long time, no hear, I been trying to get a hold of you to no avail. I know you living in the fast lane, betta slow down before you run into a brick wall. (smile) But anyway, they just transferred me to Ryan Corrections on Mound Rd. So you should slide up here and check ya boy out, it's been a year since I seen you. We past due, you can put whatever going on in the streets on hold for a minute. Besides I don't know what you searching for, you won't find another nigga like me. And that's on some real shit. Well I'm a end on that note, get back with me, I'm not use to chasing.

Love,

Don

"Man, I ain't got time for that shit," Dana balled the letter up and threw it away without a second thought. Damn, if Don only knew, the word "ride" wasn't in her vocabulary. The loyalty and respect Don displayed to her didn't mean a thing. The little sympathy or love she did have, died out long ago, not purposely but the game had swallowed her whole. They say true love withstands over time, but as an adolescent lust can be mistaken for love. Don was just convenient at the time, an asset who turned into a liability until something sweeter came along. Dana was 20 years old and moving 100 miles and running. In the wake of the new millennium, she was a seasoned vet in what we called sack-chasing, another word for gold digging. The allure of the game had her hooked like any other hustler. The past few years had been good to her, she gained weight in all the right places. No one would argue that she was a dime, everyone fell in love with her complexion, skin the color of latte. She had the body of a video vixen. All this was used to her advantage, her apartment in the River Place was paid for the next 6 months, closet full of the finest. She sat in her 2001 Impala fixing herself up in the mirror, adjusting her platinum Cartier frames with transitional tent, when the sunlight hit them, the lens change color. Her phone rung interrupting her makeup session.

"Shit, who is this calling now, Hello?"

"Girl hurry yo ass up before I change my mind," the male voice on the other line spoke loudly.

"Here I come, what mall you at?"

"Fairlane."

"Alright, I'm on my way baby, shit I ain't never turned down nothing but my collar. I hope this nigga ain't cheap." Dana said speaking on another one of her shopping sprees.

"What's happening Bobby Joe?"

"Rome my man, what's happening? You got something for me?"

"You know it, take this shit off my hands before I throw it in the air.'

119

"Ok boss, ok let's see what you got."

Rome stood behind the bulletproof glass counter with a black bookbag full of singles. Mike, the arab who owned the liquor store on Meldrum & Gratiot had known him since he was a whipper snapper. Mike knew his whole family and watched him grow up, so the love was genuine. Rome stood there and watched Mike as he rubber-banded all the singles. Mike had one foot in the street, so this was nothing new to him, in fact this was small change.

"Whatsup with you man, you suppose to have this shit sorted out already, don't get sloppy on me."

"I know Mike, my bad, I was rushing, plus I just picked all this up."

"How much is it?"

"$5,200"

"$5,200! Shit started to pick up for you huh?"

"Nah, same ol same ol for real."

"Look at you, always humble pie," Mike said as he patted Rome on his shoulder, keep it that way. Most of the other stores still stacked up, plus I still got singles from your last batch. But I'm a do it for you anyway, wait right here."

"Rome, I just left around the corner at your spot, ain't nobody there." Nene, a fiend from the neighborhood told him as soon as she walked in the store and spotted him behind the counter.

"I know auntie, it's gone be a minute."

"You don't have nothing on you?"

"Nope."

"Damn!"

Mike came back with $5,200 in big bills and handed it to Rome. "Here."

"Just give me the five, you take the two."

Mike protested as Rome got in his 2001 Yukon Denali and sped off. At nineteen, Rome felt like he found his niche, hustling was in his blood line, it came natural to him. He'd been around it all his life and he felt like he was destined. That night he asked his mother to help him get rid of the 500 grams she cursed him and told him to get the hell out of her house. She knew the game like the back of her hand, but her anger convinced her to let him learn the hard way. Rome took the cocaine to his closest oldhead since Donte was killed, Ronnie Moe. Ronnie Moe gave him $10,000 for the coke, which he used most of to help with Don's lawyer. The game is to be sold, not to be told, and with all the game Ronnie Moe would later school him too, he'd might as well gave him that work free of charge. Thanks to Ronnie Moe, Rome knew how to cook, cut and press cocaine. He knew the difference between shine and bullshit. Shine is what we called good, A-1 cocaine because of the way the scales shined in the inside when you cracked the brick open. He knew real good coke was light yellowish, not white, suckers fell for white and that's how he got them everytime. They say it's not what you know, but who you know. Rome was living proof of this, by observing and knowing the right people, he had surpassed people who'd been hustling for years.

"If you don't have a Pyrex around, and you have to use a jar always run a little cold water on it first before you start cooking, this keep the jar from cracking on you. When you whipping it, always catch it at the top. See I'm old school, I like to use a coat hanger, but you can use what you want. You'll never guess who taught me how to cook, your moms, yup, she was a beast over the stove."

Rome sat in his truck in a daze reflecting on what Ronnie Moe taught him a few years back as he thought about his mom. In six months, she'll be released from serving an 18 month bid for a trafficking charge. He'd came a long way since then, she knew it too, but he couldn't wait until she came home to see how she readjust to society, keep her promise of staying clean. His phone rung interrupting his thoughts.

"Where you at?" the voice on the other line asked.

"I'm outside why? You questioning me like you the boss or something."

"Man, you know I'm a young boss in the making."

At fifteen Jamal was cocky just like his father Donte. With his father gone and a mother who stayed in the streets, more than the speed bumps, Jamal begin running wild at age twelve. His mother Meka was more concerned with Jeans & Moet or Dress 2 Sweat night at the club than her own kids. Jamal took on a bigger role in the house and had to grow up fast. With Donte gone,

Rome filled the void for him. Not only was Jamal family, but Rome felt like he was obligated to look out for Jamal as Donte did for him when he was young. More importantly, he took a liking to Jamal and the feeling was mutual. Rome wanted to see Jamal on the right path, but he was a rebel. At first, he was in the streets on some dumb shit, stealing cars, breaking into homes, none of the scare tactics or pep talks worked to set him straight. So Rome just kept him under his wing, he figured, if he was gone be in the game anyway, he might as well deal with him, at least that way he could keep close tabs and make sure he was good.

"Yeah whatever little nigga, I'm walking in now." Rome responded before clicking his phone shut.

"1-2, 1, 1-2, 3, 1-2, 4," Don counted under his breath as he took his frustration out on the pull-up bar. His mind was all over the place, Dana still hadn't got back with him, plus he was at a new prison and he was just on edge period. Instantly he realized there was a lot of money to be made and he wanted in.

"Damn boy you going hard on that bar ain't you?" Speedy commented. They called him Speedy because he use to talk fast when he was younger and he was a motor mouth. He stayed in the mix, and kept his ear to the street, always knew what was going on but was never involved. The Jerry Springer type, all talk, no show, Don only kept him around because he was from the hood.

"Hey, when you think you gone be ready for me?" Don asked referring to the last package he had to get rid of before he got down with Don. Don noticed that Speedy's attention was elsewhere, so he followed his eyes. On the other side of the yard, near the weight bench Charlie from Brightmoor could be heard doing what he do best, running his mouth. Charlie was getting money and he wanted everybody to know it. He was a couple years older than Don, and real cocky, but he paid his dues, he had the right to be.

"C'mon man everything I touch go platinum, all my spots do Will Smith numbers. Ask about me, I am Brightmoor, and it don't stop there. I'm everywhere, see yall niggas know what I want yall to know and see what I want yall to see." Charlie had an audience, which was all the ammunition he needed.

"Hey Charlie what about ol boy Rome and then, him and Dre got a spot over there doing a little something on that block right off Fenkell & Evergreen." One of the young bucks in the circle of dudes asked him.

"Who the fuck is Rome?"

"You know Rome, Dre man from the Eastside, he drive the black Denali."

In Detroit, the east and westside were like two different worlds. It was disrespectful for somebody from the eastside to eat on the west and vice versa. It was like a unwritten code that was always broken. Some respected the game, others dealt with it accordingly, but many lives were lost behind it.

"Oh you talking bout them little niggas, they ain't no threat. Rome rode in on Dre's back, that's only cause Dre family from Brightmoor. Them boys ain't doing no real numbers, they still riding American cars. My team don't get behind the wheel unless it's

124

something foreign, Nissans & Toyotas don't count, real talk, check my resume."

By this time, Don and Speedy were fully tuned in to Charlie's rant from a distance. Don had been listening since the first mention of Rome's name. On the surface you couldn't tell how mad he was, but if this was a cartoon, smoke would be seen coming from his head and ears.

"Yeah them niggas stay in they lane, they don't do much. I let them niggas get a taste, but I don't let them feed they face. They get just enough to hold them over, know what I mean?" Charlie continued, while smirking at the same time.

Don and Speedy begin walking towards Charlie and his entourage. Don's stride and expression spoke volumes, it was obvious he meant business. Speedy was more walking on eggshells. The nigga was spooked, he knew Charlie had a long reach, but he also knew Don didn't give a fuck.

"Hey cuz, let me holla at you right quick." Don asked Charlie interrupting him.

"I ain't your cuz, and do I know you nigga?"

"Slow down tough guy, I just need a minute of your time."

"Speak up playboy, time is money."

"Step into my office, I don't like talking in front of crowds."

"Say what you gotta say, this all fam right here." Charlie was being arrogant, truth is, most of these dudes was just trying to be down and he didn't know them that well.

"Oh yeah, well check this out, keep my brother Rome name out your mouth from here on out. You speaking on shit you don't know nothing about." The surrounding crowd grew silent in anticipation.

"Picture that, picture Charlie letting another nigga tell me who and what I can talk about. Especially a nothing, nothing like you. Nothing for nothing means nothing, and nigga you's a nothing – nothing. Bum ass nigga, get the fuck out of here." Charlie countered with a cocky grin on his face, his entourage started to giggle.

"Fuck that shit Don, let's get up out of here," Speedy finally spoke up gesturing for Don to leave.

Don turned around as if he was about to leave, but spun around and stole on Charlie. Don connected right across the jaw and it let off a loud pop, Charlie fell instantly. Don connected three more times while Charlie was on the ground before his crew collapsed on him. They was on Don's ass like flies on shit. He was holding his own for a minute before he hit the ground and bawled up. These boys were trying to stomp a mudhole in Don. The CO's let it go on for awhile before they called for backup. Speedy was long gone, only thing left of him was the smoke trail he left behind. He took off when Don threw the first punch, he didn't want no parts. Charlie stood in the midst of the beating with his face all swole up and a street knife in his hand. Next thing you know Don felt two sharp pains in his side and one in his chest, then it was lights out.

126

Chapter 18

2003

"It's more to this shit than just putting it in a bag and standing there. You gotta have character and finesse in this game. Fiends are regular people and they wanna be treated like it, you trying to beat them up over 5 or 10 dollars. Disrespecting them everytime they come through, don't nobody wanna deal with that. What's wrong with yall niggas? Believe me I wouldn't tell yall or put yall through nothing, I ain't been through. I really lived this shit, same spot for days, same clothes for weeks. Not on no corny shit just saying it cause it sound good, but the spot was jumping, I couldn't leave to change clothes, couldn't leave to eat, muthafucka wanna come see me, they gotta come to me, I ain't going nowhere. It only take one time for them fiends to see the spot empty and they going somewhere else. I'm hungry, I send somebody to the store to get me some food. I'm not leaving under no circumstances, this shit is serious, treat it like your job. Don't nothing come easy. I wanna see yall come up, I don't want yall hustling for me forever. We a team, everybody gotta play they position." Rome's group of hungry young workers were all ears, they were eating up every word. He spoke so passionately and besides that, his resume added up.

Jamal sat at the table burning the tips on the bags as he watched and listened to Rome kick game to him and the five other workers that were present. When Rome talked, they listened, and why wouldn't they? He showed and proved and didn't break promises. Rome had three crackhouses with six workers, each worker was paid $500 a week and the week of the first there pay doubled to a $1000. Rome did numbers all year round

127

because he played fair. He dropped his cocaine to the oils and in whatever neighborhood, he was in he made sure his bags doubled the size of the competition.

Rome: "Hold on man, let me explain it to them, cause you don't know nothing about the game and you fucking up. Around this time my plug was consistent, but he wasn't strong. He wasn't dumping nothing on me, but he would work with me, if I ever was short. I grew up around plenty connects, but I wanted to find my own way, plus I didn't want the same shit them niggas flooded the hood with. For this, they respected me and that would soon pay off. My work was A-1 and it was jumping out the water, which means it was bouncing on its own without me whipping it. I dropped it to the oils and still got 150 grams out of every big (4 ½). This came back to about 44 ounces out of every bird. No matter what I was selling out of each spot, nickels, dimes, tre's, twenties, I made sure I only cut $960 out of each ounce. After paying the workers and sucking up whatever losses, I'll end up with $650-700 off of every ounce. So, I was bringing back like $32,000 off a bird, getting them for $19,500, I was pushing them out the door in like 4 or 5 days. $13,000 profit a week was good money for a nigga like me at the time. I had never seen nothing like it and eventhough I tried to humble myself, slowly but surely it started to show. Acting like a nigga that ain't never had shit."

Rio: "Damn, you sure talk a lot for a person who trying to dodge indictments."

Rome: "Ah man, I don't know what you talking bout, this is fiction, not fact." (Rome says with a smile)

Rio: "Yeah al-right, well let me get back to my job then."

****

"No this nigga didn't, dog I know this nigga just didn't drop that new 645i, I just seen that thing at the Auto Show down at Cobo. That mug just dropped. Yo Ski is that the "03?" Tone asked as Ski pulled up on the block showing off the newest toy to his collection.

"Is it water in a toilet? C'mon man you already know." Ski answered arrogantly. A red bone followed behind and parking driving his black 745il.

"C'mon baby, get out we going to the store right quick?"

"Alright I'm following you," she responded.

"Naw girl, get out we walking its right down the block."

She opened the door unaware and hesitant about her surroundings. The look on her face told you she wasn't use to the hood or the treatment she was receiving. She shook her head before stepping out in a Chanel dress that stopped about 3 inches above her knees with the matching purse and sandals. All eyes were on here, she looked like Cassie except with the body of video vixen Esther Baxter.

"Ski, what about my girls?"

"They cool, they in good hands." This caught the fellas off guard because they didn't realize it was more than one other female in the car with her. The

129

curtains inside the 745 concealed their faces in the backseat. The fellas shifted their focus back to the whip.

"Hey little Rome everybody know you getting a couple dollars now, when you gone boss up and get you one of these foreign toys." Ski shouted as he walked through the lot towards the store with his lady friend.

Rome just shook his head and smirked, but his attention was elsewhere. Every since the curtains were peeled back, his eyes were fixated on the backseat. At this moment, him and the young lady were playing the cat and mouse game. You know she catch him looking, he look away, he catch her looking, she look away. At the moment the fellas were smothering the car, it wasn't his style to be competing with a bunch of dudes or breaking his neck to get a females attention, but those cat like eyes were calling him. Her face was immaculate, she looked like a younger version of the actress Sana Lathan. Rome didn't care if she got out the car with a 300lb frame, her facial beauty alone had him mesmerized. His phone rung interrupting their staring match, he was so off balance, he answered the wrong phone. She peeped it and smiled as he reached for his other one.

"Yeah whatsup," Rome answered.

"Where you at boy?" It was his man's Dre with a bunch of music in the background. "What you got up for the night?"

"Nothing why, whatsup?"

"I already checked on Brightmoor, I got some hoes lined up, meet me downtown at the Good Life."

"Alright bet, I gotta go meet Will first though," Rome answered speaking of his connect.

When he hung up the phone, his newfound friend was waving goodbye as the 745 pulled off. He was salty, but he didn't let it show, he made a mental note to get with Ski A.S.A.P. so he can get with her.

Inside the 745, it was a lot of conversation. "Girl bout time your ass start flirting with somebody at least, Antonio don't have eyes everywhere, I want the old Andrea back."

"Tia shutup, wasn't nobody flirting."

Tia mashed the brakes, hit the steering wheel, turned around and looked Andrea dead in the eye. "Who you think you fooling!!" Andrea and the rest of the girls burst out laughing.

"So what, you want me to tell Ski to hook you up?"

"I don't know if I'm ready yet Tia, plus he look kind of young."

"Yeah whatever, all you gotta do is say the word. That young nigga sexy as hell, did you see them dimples?"

****

Back in Ryan Correctional Facility

Charlie strutted across the tier during block out, like he was the best thing since the triple beam. Stabbing Don and sending him to an outside hospital

131

only fueled his arrogance. If it wasn't for one of the CO's he had on the payroll stopping him, he'd be buried in the hole right now, with a homicide. His face was a little swole, but he didn't give a fuck, he got the last laugh.

"Yeah baby play with that pussy for me, let me know you miss me........."

"Nigga I'm ready, you can stop acting like you on the phone now." Charlie said to one of his flunkies who was holding the phone down for him. "Here." Charlie handed him a pack of Newports as the man passed him the phone.

"Whatsup cuz?" the voice on the line answered after accepting the charges.

"What's the deal, you got that info for me?" Charlie asked.

"Oh yeah, you know that's already in motion, I'm just waiting on the OK."

"Yeah go head and take care of that, these little niggas need to know who they dealing with.'

"Fa sho," the voice replied.

Charlie hung up the phone with a slight grin on his face rubbing his palms together.

****

The Good Life Bar & Lounge downtown on Woodward Ave had a nice crowd, Jay-Z's new single "Change Clothes" filled the speakers in the background.

132

Dre stepped outside the bar to use the phone to see what was taking Rome so long.

"Whatsup dog, where you at?"

"Man chill, I'm pulling up now."

"Nigga quit fronting, I'm outside, somebody just pulled up in that new Audi A8 you always talking bout, platinum gray, it's looking good too."

Rome pulled to a stop in front of the Good Life. He was grinning like a kid in a candy store. Ronnie Moe was in the passenger seat, smoking a el about as long as a No. 2 pencil. "Roleys don't tic toc" by the local group the "Street Lords" could be heard pumping out the system.

"Oh yeah, that's how you feeling!" Dre shouted. And you pull up playing my shit too. Don't do nothing to him, leave him just like that. That thing cost $80,000, let them niggas have them rims, TV's and shit."

"You ain't gotta tell me how to ride dog, I been at this shit for a minute," Rome replied.

"I know you ain't cash him out?"

"Mind your business nigga, hey, I'm bout to go park, I'll be in there in a minute. I'm feeling good so I hope you got something in there nice for me." Rome stated referring to the females Dre had waiting inside. Rome hit the button to pop the trunk as he was parallel parking the Audi. When you shut the V-12 engine off it's like you could actually feel the car lowering itself to the ground. Rome made his way to the trunk to retrieve

Ronnie Moe's wheelchair, he had been paralyzed for the past 2 ½ years. He caught a bad deal after a shootout with Geno and his team. Even after Geno realized that his sister (Meka) was actually the person who contacted the authorities, his on-going feud with the hood continued. Stoney ended up copping out to 10 – 20 years for manslaughter, Ronne Moe couldn't get to him, so he felt someone had to pay. About twenty shootings and a thousand shells later, Ronnie Moe was in a wheelchair with about 12 bodies under his belt. Anytime somebody gave him a sorrowful look due to his disability, he always hit them with the popular saying, (as if he was in a fight) "you should see the other niggas."

"If you don't get no pussy tonight something wrong." Ronnie Moe commented as he led the way in his motorized wheelchair. In a wheelchair Ronnie Moe was probably one of the freshest dudes you'd see on the planet. Tonight he kept it basic with a navy blue cotton Polo sweat suit and a pair of navy blue alligator print Mauri kicks. His Franck Muller watch had crush diamonds around the bezel. Despite his handicap, he partied hard and lived his life to the fullest. If he had any insecurities, he didn't let it show, besides special occasions, the only time he really went out was with Rome.

When Rome entered the Good Life he spotted Dre in the back with two bottles of Dom Perigon on the table. Dre was stunting hard, he was the flashy type, if you didn't know him, his lingo and swagger would have you thinking he was filthy rich.

"She ain't never had Dom before, I thought I'd be the first to break her in." Dre stated as Rome was sitting, Rome just nodded with a slight smile.

"Shaniyah this my man Rome, Rome this Shaniyah." Dre introduced them. They both gave each other the once over, Shaniyah made her mind up right then and there that she was gonna give Rome some pussy. If his talk matched his look, yup, he'd be a winner tonight.

"Whatsup Shaniyah Dre got you in here by yourself tonight?"

"Nah my girl in the bathroom why, were you expecting somebody?"

"You silly, nah believe me you already exceeded my expectations."

That was corny, but it made Shaniyah blush anyway. "Yeah ok, it sound good."

"It is good."

"Yeah, we'll see," Shaniyah responded as she stuck her tongue out slightly and licked her top lip seductively.

Before that Rome wasn't even interested, but now she had his full attention. Shaniyah wasn't really his type, off first glance he realized she was a high class hoodrat. She kept checking her phone like someone was calling her, checking the time when she should of owned a watch to serve that purpose. Plus she was eyeing his key-ring trying to see what kind of car he drove.

135

"Damn baby bout time I thought you might of needed some help in there." Dre asked Dana as she was approaching the table. Dana was shocked to see him accompanied by Rome. "Damn it's a small world, how you know this nigga? Oh I forgot you get around now huh Rome?" Dana stated arrogantly.

"You know my man Rome?" asked Dre.

"Yup me and Rome go way back before he got his little gangster persona. Ain't that right Rome?"

"You must got me confused with somebody else cause I don't know you."

"Boy shutup and stop playing with me," Dana said laughing as she threw a napkin in Rome's face. The whole table erupted in laughter, the ice was broken and everybody started vibing.

"Ronnie Moe whatsup why you so quiet, what you drinking my nigga?" Dre asked as him and Rome made their way to the bar. "Damn dog, where you know Dana from, that bitch a freak!! She out cold with it, I'm telling you, when I say, she do it all, I mean she do it all. I know her girl with it, yo we at the room tonight."

"Damn dog, slow down you act like you ain't never had no pussy."

"Shutup nigga, you know I'm buzzing."

"Me and Dana grew up together, I ain't seen her in awhile, but she good people." Rome kept it simple and left out there history. "Hell nah, look who in here," he stated looking towards the restroom. Omar was walking like he had way too many shots. He was under the table for real, which was an old-school slang term used in Detroit meaning drunk.

"Damn that nigga slipping, I should get at him right now."

"Get at him for what?"

"What you mean get at him for what?" Rome looked at Dre with his face frowned up. "Man it's been five years since my man got killed on his turf and this nigga still don't have no answers. I'm starting to think he had something to do with it, grab the bottles I be back I'm going to holler at him." Rome entered the restroom.

"Whatsup playboy, I see you feeling good." Omar had his back turned washing his hands.

"Who dat?"

"Nigga turn your drunk ass around so you can see." Omar turned around with his hands in his pants as if he was reaching for his mag.

"Boy you betta chill, you almost caught something hot."

"Oh yeah." Omar was smiling, but Rome kept his face straight as if he missed the joke.

"Whatup doe? You see all them hoes out there." Omar stated.

"Whatsup dog, why you ain't never get back at me?"

"On what tip?"

"C'mon man you said you had got word on that situation."

"Oh yeah, I'm still working on it, I'm definitely gone keep you posted homie. I think about little cuz everyday, that shit be eating me up."

"Yeah, I hear you talking, on some real shit 'O' you starting to look suspect my nigga." At this time, they were looking each other directly in the eye.

"Fuck you mean by that dog?" Omar asked taking a step closer in Rome's direction. By this time they had gained the attention of a few bystanders in the restroom.

"It mean whatever you want it to mean my guy."

Omar just smirked turning his back to Rome as he made his way to the exit. "You know, don't let them little couple dollars you touching go to your head, you getting a little too big for your bridges." Dre walked in on the tail end of the conversation.

"You cool cuz? Ronnie Moe want me to take him to the car and everything, whatsup?"

Chapter 19

"They got fence surrounding the inside of every window except for the two back ones on the left hand side. Its two workers and a runner in there right now. The nigga Lil Butch and Corey in there, ol boy Jamal stop through a lot, but he just left."

"Ok, ok, slow your roll up homeboy." Big T, Charlie's right hand man interrupted the teenager as he gave him the rundown on two of Rome's crackhouses. Big T already had the inside scoop on how Rome ran his operation, he was just picking the young fellas brain. Lil Curt use to work for Rome, but he kept running off with the sack, so Rome fired him before he became a casualty.

"So what you get fired for little nigga, you was stealing wasn't you." Big T asked.

"Man, I ain't no thief!!! Rome got rid of me cause I was from the Westside and I kept getting into it with them Eastside niggas he had working. You know they don't like us for real, Dre was on some bullshit too, dicksucking, so I just rolled out."

"So what you wanna get back at them?" Big T asked knowing his story was some bullshit.

"Fa sho."

"Get in right quick, we taking a ride."

["These are my confessions, I done it all, said all I could say, my chick on the side, say she got one on the

139

way. Man I'm tired and I don't know what to do, I guess I gotta give part II of my confessions."]

Usher thumped through the speakers, nine bottles and five blunts later, the foursome was the life of the party. Every song played was their jam and Shaniyah was starting to look like a runway model.

"You might not be able to keep up with me tonight, look I got you excited already." Shaniyah spoke in a whisper grabbing Rome's dick while grinding on him. She wasn't the best looker, but she had the body of a goddess, you'd think they made the song brickhouse just for her.

"You putting your hand on it, like it's yours," Rome commented basically just standing on the dance floor. His two-step had become nonexistent, all he could think of was what was between those juicy thighs.

"After tonight it will be."

"You sure about that?"

"Positive, I got them A-1's," she said with a devilish grin.

Ronnie Moe was posted in the corner with a half empty bottle in his hand talking to a female he knew from back in the day in his "Dancery" days, a local club on Mt. Elliot. Ronnie Moe clutched the bottle eventhough he didn't drink anymore. He was always cautious, but due to his handicap, he felt like he couldn't afford to drink. He already was at a disadvantage so he felt he had to be ten steps ahead at all times, funny, considering he was in a wheelchair.

"Hey yo Dre, Dre!!" Ronnie Moe shouted over the music as Dre whispered something in Dana's ear. "Hey man tell Rome I'm bout to get up out of here. I'm sliding with her tonight, shit its bout that time for yall to be stepping too ain't it?"

"Great minds think alike, I'm already on it my nigga."

****

The Expedition bent the corner on Burt Rd. & Fenkell for the third time. It was one in the morning, but it was late August, in the ghetto so the streets were still bustling. Big T didn't care if people noticed his truck, he wanted the streets to know who was behind what he was about to do. He was about to show them why they called Charlie the governor of Brightmoor and him the mayor. Lil Curt sat in the backseat zoned out listening to Big Herk (a local rapper from Detroit) album rapping every song word for word on some amp shit. ("Push rock in Saginaw, sold stones in Flint, my Nextel was tapped, so I got a phone from Sprint.") He was off two ecstasy pills, double stacks, chasing it with purple haze and water. Those drugs combined had him feeling invincible, he felt like Scarface at the end of the movie when he took all them gunshots.

"I wet who you wanted wetted, you wet who I want wetted, any nigga can get it." Lil Curt sang along as the CD changer switched to Nas.

"Whatsup I'm ready to off all them niggas!!" Lil Curt shouts biting his bottom lip shaking his head.

Big T just smirked as he parked the truck two houses down in a miscellaneous driveway. "Ay yo, we

141

here, yall in position?" Big T asked speaking into his Nextel chirp.

"Yep we ready, when you ready, soon as lil dog leave out, we on it," the voice answered through the chirp.

Big T hopped out the truck with a M-16, yeah I said it, the dude had a M-16 with 30 round bursts, setting up right across the street. The passenger and Lil Curt were making their way to the house with two 4-5's with extended 25 shot clips. All this wasn't necessary for the spot, but they were giving Rome and Dre the benefit of the doubt, you never knew what was waiting on you behind those doors.

Johnie the runner looked through the peephole surprised and cautious that somebody was beating on the front door since all the traffic was ran through the back.

"I'll be damned, look what the cat done drug in, it's gone be hell to tell the captain this one!" Johnie said as he was opening the door for Lil Curt. "I must of talked your ass up cause I was ……"

"Bloc! Bloc!! Lil Curt wasted no time, call him the microwave killer, do is shit instantly. He emptied the rest of his 25 shot clip into Lil Butch and Corey, they layed slump with shocked facial expressions still on their faces from witnessing Johnie get murked. As if he just didn't commit a triple homicide, Lil Curt walked over to the glass table and finished off the cheeseburger deluxe that Corey was eating. The mixture of the drugs had his thought process twisted, he could have been in the next ad for a "this is your brain on drugs commercial."

142

"Yo T, what the fuck taking this nigga so long, I been heard the shots." The leader of the group in the box Chevy Caprice spoke through the Nextel to Big T, in the backseat on the floor were homemade Molotov cocktails with tide detergent.

"Fuck that little nigga, stick to the plan and follow my lead." Big T positioned himself directly in front of the house and let the M-16 roar, "Rat, tat, tat, tat, tat, the 30-round per minute bursts sounded like a 100 people were tap dancing at the same time. The few people who stuck around on the block to be nosy had got the hell out of dodge. The Chevy Caprice pulled up and firebombed the home with Molotov cocktails. Playing both sides of the fence, trying to be down, in way over his head, all these factors led to Lil Curt's demise. A firebombing with three dead bodies was overkill, these boys were trying to send a message. I guess Charlie was Mr. Brightmoor?

****

Meanwhile, downtown at the Marriot Hotel in the Renaissance Center, Dre set the temperature on the Jacuzzi as the girls got comfortable. They didn't even care that the guys got one room with two beds, it was no shame in their game.

"Hey yo Dre let me see one of them room keys, I gotta make a run right quick."

"Where you going to get you some ginseng?" Shaniyah said amusing herself.

"Yeah whatever I see you got jokes"

143

"Where you going dog?" Dre asked Rome in a low whisper.

"Nigga you got some rubbers?"

"All damn, I only got two.'

"Well, I'm bout to go to the gas station right quick to grab some. Yall want something?"

"Nah just bring yourself back and I'm cool." Shaniyah said sitting on the bed with her shoes off and her legs cocked open. Dana and Dre were in the corner tongue kissing.

"Damn dog you don't know where her mouth been."

"Boy shutup," Dana states throwing the pillow at him.

"I don't put my mouth on nothing that don't belong to me."

Rome pulled up to the Amoco station on Jefferson across the street from the Comfort Inn, he got there in like sixty seconds doing almost fifty in bumper to bumper traffic. He had pussy on the brain mixed with heavy champagne and weed. He parks his Audi next to the door and gets out with the car still running.

"Let me get two boxes of magnums."

"Wait one second, I already started ringing someone up," the Arab clerk said from behind the counter.

It was hard for Rome to contain the shock on his face when he turned around and looked at who stood before him. The same angelic face that captivated him 3 days prior in the backseat of Ski's 745. He stood there and took in what he wasn't able to witness when she was sitting from a distance, which was her style and her physique. Her body was the perfect compromise, she was petite but not too skinny, very healthy looking. Her behind was round and stuck out due to her slight bowleg. Bottom line, her body was banging, perfectly proportioned. He looked her from head to toe and admired her style. Her low-cut Gucci loafers with printed G's all over them matched her purse to a tee and they also accentuated the tan stitching in her BCBG denim jean set.

"I see you still have a staring problem." Andrea said as she stood there with two family size bags of Doritos in her hand while the cashier rung up the rest of her goodies.

Rome just laughed it off, "You know I didn't have you as the junk food type."

Andrea sighed as she responded, "I didn't have you as the slutty type." She says eyeing the two boxes of condoms as she makes her way out the door. She didn't give Rome time to respond as she got in her car and sped off.

Minutes later, Rome ended up catching her at the light bobbing her head to the music in her drop-top lavender Jaguar XJR. Automatically he knew she wouldn't be impressed by his Audi A8, but in fact she was, it showed he had class and wasn't the average young guy following what he seen on a rap video. She caught him looking and rolled down the window.

"What I tell you about staring?"

"Maybe I like what I see."

"Ok, so what you gone do about it?"

And just then the light changed, Rome's attempt to follow her were cut short by a van making a left turn.

"Sniff, sniff, sniff….." Dana imitated a vacuum cleaner as she snorted her second line of cocaine. She lifted her head up from the nightstand and tweaked her nose with her thumb and index finger catching the drain.

"Damn baby slow down on that shit, you been going hard all night." Dre commented, sitting on the bed in his boxers.

"Boy be quiet, plus you know this shit have me feeling like Janet, Ms. Jackson if you nasty."

Dre would agree with anything Dana said right now, with her standing there in a cream lace bra and panty set. Dana took her first tote at a party full of high rollers while dating a major player from the northeast side of Detroit. Her infatuation with the lifestyle led her to follow suit and she has been snorting ever since.

"Dana come on over here to mama so we can get this party started." Shaniyah stated grinning as she stood next to Dana in a black negligee gripping her left butt cheek. She placed soft kisses on her startling her.

"Girl what are you doing?" Dana jumped with a silly grin on her face.

"Oh, so you gone act brand new on me now? It's all good, I know what I gotta do." Shaniyah squatted as she placed soft kisses all over her lower body, starting from her behind to her thighs and calf's. In the same motion, she slid Dana's lace panties to the side while inserting her finger in her moist opening. Dana jumps slightly as she backs up and positioning herself at the foot of the dresser.

"Damn baby, you soaking," Shaniyah says as she works her fingers in and out and massages Dana's nipples with her other hand. "You must miss me huh baby? Huh? I can't hear you tell me you miss me?"

"Ummm Hmm Hmmm…" Dana moaned.

"I can't hear you?"

Dre sat there in awe as he witnessed the unexpected and every man's fantasy. His hand was on his dick as he battled with the idea of playing with himself or just barging in.

"C'mere baby, lay down for mama," Shaniyah led Dana to the bed opposite Dre. Dana felt like she was floating on air as she laid down on her back with her legs slightly arched. Instantly Shaniyah put her tongue ring to work. She spreads her pussy lips wide as she teased Dana sticking her tongue in and out while simultaneously sucking the clit.

"Ohhh Ahhh ahhh ohhh shit.." Dana moaned as she squirmed and held Shaniyah's head for dear life. Shaniyah has her hands cupped underneath Dana's

147

thighs and each time she jumped Shaniyah pulled her back.

"Uh huh, where you going, don't run from it."

Rome walked in on the middle of the sexcapade and was so shocked he thought he had the wrong room. "Damn that's how they feeling," he said to Dre as more of a statement than a question,. Dre hopped up in his boxers with his hands covering his bulge.

"You already know, I told you I had something nice for you."

The ladies hadn't missed a beat and was still going at it. Dana was approaching her third orgasm. "Baby what are you doing to me, ohh, please stop, please (screaming) Ahhh!! Ahhh!!! Ohh!"

"Damn dog you playing with your nose now?" Rome asked looking towards the nightstand.

"Hell naw, that's all them."

"Dana was fucking with that shit too?"

"Shit that's Dana's package."

That threw Rome for a loop, he didn't see that coming, but as he thought back to the bar, that's why she was in and out the restroom all night. "Damn," he said aloud to himself. He made a mental note that he would keep her close so they could go visit Don first thing in the morning.

"C'mon baby, you next," Shaniyah said fiddling with his zipper breaking his train of thought.

Ryan Correctional

"Folsom!! Let's go, pack it up!! Don gathered the belongings he'd accumulated while recovering in the infirmary. The prison staff tried their hardest to convince him to stay in lock up, they didn't want him back in general population, but Don seen through all there tactics. Everything from were concerned about your safety, or we'll make your life a living hell here, your ass a never go home. Take it as a blessing, a couple more inches and your lung would have needed to be removed, is what the nurse told him. Don reflected on all these things as the CO escorted him back to his housing unit. The thoughts only fueled his hunger for retaliation, all eyes were on him as he approached his cell.

"Whatup doe?" his cellmate greeted him when he walked in. Don just looked at him and got on the bunk, disregarding him speaking. This was out of character for him, but he was on edge, besides, what you expect after he just got jumped and stabbed up in front of almost the whole prison. His cellmate realized this and just sat back giving Don his space.

****

Eastside Detroit

"Bet back, bet back on the 6-8 too. Whatsup scared money, don't make money. Oh yeah this shit feel good too." Jamal closed his palm and shook the dice rapidly. "Yall know what, I'm full than a muthafucka,...cause I just eight!!! Pickup big Mal, he said after he hit his second eight. This shit about to get ugly." Jamal stated before answering the phone. Rome

149

was on the other end talking loud and cursing. "I'm out of here dog, hey Sweets here; Jamal gave the house man a generous tip before leaving.

"Damn Mal, you just gone hit the dice game and leave huh? You disrespectful cuz." Fat Mike a grimy dude from North End said what everyone else was thinking. It was only right since he lost the most money.

"I'm a working man, what you want me to do?"

"Bitch as nigga….," Fat Mike says under his breath.

The rain was pouring down so hard it looked like a small hurricane was forming, Rome sat three houses down from his spot on Lakewood & Canfield deep in thought. The lighting from the digital dash and touchpad screen above the console illuminated the Audi. Even through the heavy rain, smoke debris could be seen in the night sky, in just a half a day his two most profitable drug spots out of the three were firebombed and burnt to a crisp. Three of his workers were killed along with their bodies being torched in Brightmoor. The streets were buzzing, homicide was snooping around, and Rome didn't have a clue.

"Who the fuck!!" he whispered under his breath as he hit the steering wheel with his fist. A black Marauder pulls up and Jamal hops out the passenger side running over to Rome's car getting in.

"Dog, what the fuck happened!!"

"If you was here, you would know what happened. What the spot doing empty dog?"

150

"Nigga I was calling you all last night, you or Dre didn't answer the phone. I even checked with Fonz and he said he was trying to get with you."

"Why you ain't go to the crib on Mt. Elliot to grab something?"

"Man c'mon now? I did that first, that shit been gone. Fuck all that though, who burnt down the spot? Who we got a problem with?"

"Dog, I don't know what's going on." Jamal gave Rome a dis-believing look.

"It could be them niggas on Dickerson off Jefferson."

"But I thought they had started shopping with you?" Jamal stated.

"Man that don't mean shit, but naw that don't really add up cause the spot in Brightmoor got torched too."

"What!!"

"Yeah, Lil Curt, Butch and Corey gone."

"They was in there?"

"Yup, homicide swarming around there because they died from multiple gunshot wounds before being burned. For the next 5-10 minutes Rome ran down the story to Jamal, everything from where he was last night to the M-16 casings that were found around the premises, letting him know whoever he was dealing with was playing for keeps. He had to brainstorm and plot his next move, something was gonna shake though most definitely.

Chapter 20

"Ohh that's my jam!" Ms. Patti yelled swinging her hips like she had a flashback from the seventies. "Shane turn that up!" "The reasons..., the reasons why we here." Earth, Wind & Fire could be heard through the speakers above the chatter and laughter. The scent of marijuana filled the air, liquor varied from fifths to gallons, coolers of beer, bottled water and soda. A sign above the fence in the backyard read, "Welcome Home Debra." Chuck handled the grill, he even got cleaned up for the festivities. His presidential Rolex was gleaming and he bought the Rolls Royce out that he barely drove. It was a 96 model, and eventhough it was 2003 he was making a statement. He was one of the only dudes on the Eastside who had the Rolls in '96', back when the average cat didn't know what it was and thought it was ugly. Only the elite knew the price and respected it to the fullest.

"You been keeping an eye on my baby?" Debra asked Chuck as he flipped the chicken breast on the grill.

"That boy a grown man, why I gotta keep an eye on him? Rome got a head on his shoulders, he gone be alright, he know what he doing."

"Yeah that's what they all think, next thing you know, they writing you letters from some prison somewhere or you making funeral arrangements."

"Well, it is what it is."

"That's all you got to say?"

"Look Debra," Chuck said looking her directly in the eye. "If you wanted him out the game, you should

153

of thought about that a long time ago. That boy 20 years old riding around in a $80,000 car, he got a little squad and some niggas who listen to him, his head too big and he too far in to listen to anybody right now. The game gotta push him out, your best bet is now that you cleaned up, is to lead by example."

Debra sat there looking puzzled. He gave it to her straight up, no chaser. That's what Chuck was known for, tough love and constructive criticism.

"Damn all I did was make one comment and you took it there." Debra said while playfully pushing Chuck on his shoulder. They both chuckled, at that instant they looked up and noticed Rome heading their way.

Rome looked his mother up and down and had never been more proud that she was the woman who birthed him. Not like he wasn't proud before, but he couldn't remember a time seeing his mother look this good. Her face was glowing and she had put all her weight back on. Skin was clear, hair and nails done, she reminded him of Whitney Houston, the clean Whitney of course.

"Boy, come hug your mama, and what took you so long?"

"You look good ma," Rome said upon releasing her.

"You do too baby. That car nice, I see you done started spending that money, you buy you a house yet?"

"I got a apartment in Novi."

"Ummm hmm, get it together Rome, you know better than that.   Who's your friend, you not gone introduce us?"

"Oh her, she ain't nobody.'

"Boy stop," Dana extended her hand, "How you doing Ms. Wilson, we met before a long time ago, you probably don't remember."

"Uh huh, girl I'm getting old, but I don't forget a face, you Don's friend right?"

Dana nodded.

"Nice seeing you again, you grew up to be a nice looking young lady, look at all these old men gawking." Dana blushed and adjusted her strapless bra under her halter top. "Yall go head and get yall some food, drinks or whatever.   They wait to I quit drinking to buy the good stuff."

"You ain't drinking nothing ma?"

"Nope, I told you, I was done, didn't I."   She looked at Rome as if it was a dumb question.

"We cool, we on our way to visit Don anyway."

Ryan Correctional

The yard on Ryan was almost filled to capacity. If there was a capacity, because in prison if there wasn't enough space, they would make some somehow. It was the beginning of fall, and everyone was out trying to enjoy the weather because it was a nice day. About 75 degrees, and all the prisoners knew this would be one of

155

the last warm days before winter came and stole their joy, so they had to enjoy it while it last. In Don's mind this was perfect timing, the more the merrier, less attention that would be directed his way. This was Don's first trip to the yard since he re-entered population, and for what he had planned it might be his last for awhile. He figured he'd let everything die down for awhile, but unbeknownst to him, his presence was felt. Although, him and Charlie were young-guns to the game, most of the population in the jail had time in, and were professionals. They seen it all before and could predict these younger cats next move with ease. Don paced the yard in layered clothing, sweat suit under his state blues, a jailhouse shank and a street knife he bought from a CO for $100. His face was screwed up, not purposely, but vengeance was on his mind and it was evident.

"Hey Don, let me holla at you." Speedy called out.

"Get the fuck out of here nigga, you just dead weight."

"Damn, that's how you feel?"

"Fuck you mean, yeah that's how I feel nigga, you left me for dead when that shit popped off, I ain't forget about that when we touch, I'm a see you!!" Speedy stood there like he was shell-shocked.

"But hold up listen......"

Don kept it moving before he could finish, he had tunnel vision right now. All he could see was sending Charlie out on the helicopter on a stretcher. He noticed a couple of the dudes who jumped him that day

156

crowded around the weight bench. Fuck the flunkies though, he wanted the big fish. They noticed Don and switched up there demeanor. Don smirked thinking to himself how soft they came across without their leader.

"Damn, where the fuck this nigga at, he don't never miss a yard." Don whispered under his breath. "Fuck it, I'm a check these niggas, send a message."

Small whispers could be heard within Charlie's homies. "Ay yo, watch this nigga, he on his way this way." "Man fuck that nigga, he ain't no threat! You got your thing on you right?" "Shit is the sky blue?" "Alright bet, cause he got his hands in his pants like he gone do something, we gone strike first though."

Don didn't know what he was walking into and he didn't give a fuck, somebody was gone feel his wrath. He approached the weight bench with one hand on his street knife tucked in his pants.

"Folsom!! 45-1967, Folsom!! 45-1967, report back to the block, visit!" The bullhorn in the yard sounded. "Folsom, visit."

"Damn!!" Don snapped as one of the guards pointed in his direction.

Minutes later, the visiting hall was crowded and full of ruckus, Don automatically assumed it was Rome as he scanned the room looking for his face. Once he spotted Dana his whole demeanor changed and he smiled for the first time in weeks.

"Hey boo, you looking good," Dana said as she stood up to hug Don.

157

"You looking better though, damn you got a little thicker too, I like that." Don let his hands explore her body. "You came up here by yourself?"

"Naw Rome brought me, he in the bathroom."

"I ain't even know yall was coming, yall could of gave a nigga a heads up."

"Why, was you expecting another bitch or something?" That brought a smile to Don's face.

"Yeah I was."

"Don't play with me Don!!"

"Whatsup my nigga." Don gave Rome a five and a hug as he walked up. Everytime Rome visited Don, they were all smiles because the love was genuine.

"What's been going on dog?" Don asked.

"Aw man, all type of crazy shit. I don't even know where to start. But we gone get into all that, but yo tell me why I come out the bathroom a few minutes ago and this nigga was mugging the shit out of me."

"Who?"

"Ol boy sitting behind you to your right, sitting with the chick and little boy, I guess that's his son or something."

Don turned around and coincidentally Charlie was staring directly at him. Don nodded his head and turned his attention back to Rome and Dana. "Hey cuz you get that letter I sent you?"

"Nope, I ain't even been to the crib in a minute, why, whatsup?"

"That's what I been meaning to holla at you about, I should of called you when I got out the hole….."

"What's going on my nigga?"

For the next twenty or twenty-five minutes, Don broke down the whole story in detail. He put emphasis on the way Charlie was running his mouth in the yard to his boys about Rome. Rome instantly put two and two together and realized Charlie was probably behind his spots getting firebombed. He heard of Charlie before, knew his resume and the way his team moved, but he was the type of dude that could careless. And, fuck him, it is what it is, everybody's expendable could describe Rome's attitude.

"So, what's your next move?" Don asked after Rome finished explaining the situation and his latest troubles. It was obvious to the both of them that Charlie was behind it.

"I can't believe you gotta ask me something like that."

(Don responded with a smile)

Meanwhile at Charlie's table, instead of taking advantage of his time with his son and baby mother Tamara, his concentration was elsewhere.

"Look at these silly ass niggas, baby, that's ol boy I told you I had to hit up a couple weeks ago." Tamara looked but really wasn't interested, she glanced to satisfy Charlie. As much as he tried to downplay their status in the game, the simple fact that he was speaking on them convinced her otherwise.

"A nigga touch a bird or two and think they big time. Then they get some drama with some real heavy hitters and be ready to leave the game alone for good."

Tamara just sat there nodding her head, giving one word answers barely listening. She cut him off. "I'm thirsty, you want something from the vending machine?"

"Naw, I'm cool, what's wrong with you?"

"Nothing!" Tamara said with attitude as she stood up. Each time she stood another pair of eyes were glued to her. Tamara had an ass you could sit a beer mug on. With every step she took her behind swayed from side to side like it had a mind of its own. Her c-cup size breasts bounced along with her stride, to some her physique could be intimidating, she favored the actress Taral Hicks, who played the role of Keisha in the movie "Belly."

"Damn, she got a motherfucking body!!" Rome commented making the sour face.

Tamara knew all eyes were on her, she made it her business to wear something provocative everytime she visited Charlie. Most women loved attention, but Tamara lived for it.

"Yo Don, pump ya brakes on ol boy for a minute. I'm a take care of it."

"Fuck you mean?"

"Dog I need you out here with me, we gone put that nigga to sleep in due time."

"Man that nigga got at least five more years left. I'm getting at him A.S.A.P. Ain't nothing you can do to change that. Ain't no use of putting no bread on his head cause all these   niggas scared or on his line."

"I know I just want you to chill cause you in here by yourself."

"Once you hit the chief, the Indians will fall, plus I got something up my sleeve."

Rome had to respect it, plus he thought about what he would do if the shoe was on the other foot. "Folsom! Twenty minutes!" The CO shouts throughout the visiting room.

"Hey, I'm a let yall kick it for these last couple minutes. I'll be back up here tomorrow my nigga. Don't worry bout nothing, be smooth. I'm a take care of everything on my end, make sure niggas feel us out there." Rome made his way out the door and gave Dana her quality time with Don.

161

Chapter 21

"Auntie you keep coming around here trying to run this same ol game. Take your ass home, you don't need to be around here fucking with this shit anyway. I don't got it over here right now, holla at me later."

"Boy you must think I was born last night, quit playing with me Omar!!"

"Damn everytime I look up you want something, how the fuck you want a lookout, wakeup and a hit."

(laughter) Omar's workers were in the background laughing their hearts out, damn near coming to tears eventhough it wasn't that funny. Omar stood on the porch of the dilapidated house making fun of his auntie literally. The house was located a few blocks from the apartment complex a.k.a. "baby carter" in Southwest Detroit. It served as a hangout / crackhouse, Omar figured since the young cats would be chilling, they might as well be counting money.

"You're a fucking disgrace, if your son was alive, he'd probably disown your ass. That's karma catching up….."

"Don't you bring my son into this shit!!" Renee snapped and tried to swing on Omar, but one of the young dudes on the porch caught her. "You dirty motherfucker, you the reason he gone motherfucker! Let me go, boy get your hands off of me!!"

"Let her go," Omar told Tory. No sooner than he released her, Renee jabbed Omar dead on his nose. Omar kicked her down the steps off natural reflex. His

162

audience burst out laughing, eventhough he was drunk and out of line.

"You gone get yours, I swear you gone get yours muthafucker!" Omar knew how to get under Renee's skin. Jake's death really opened her eyes to the fact that she was unfit as a parent. Her conscious ate at her daily, and nowadays it was hard for her to look at herself in the mirror. The reality of losing her son before she really got a chance to get to know him was too much to bear. When laying on her back with a different man every night could no longer suppress her pain, sad to say, she turned to the glass dick. Back in the day, Renee turned heads due to her natural beauty, now people did double takes because they couldn't believe it was her.

Directly down the block, Rome sat in his Audi watching the whole scene unfold. He couldn't hear a word neither were saying, but there body language spoke volumes. Fresh off his usual routine from visiting Jake, his emotions were running high. Word got to him through the street that Renee had started smoking, but this was his first time bearing witness. Rome hadn't seen her since last Oct., little did he know she was a closet smoker then. He cruised up the street to catch up with Renee as she stormed up the block stomping her feet.

"Ma you alright, slow down, ma slow down for a minute," he shouts out the window.

"Leave me alone I ain't doing nothing right now." Renee responds without looking automatically assuming Rome was a trick.

"Ma it's me Rome! Hurry and get in, you know this block hot."

"Who?"

"Rome." Rome pulled the car over as Renee squinted her eyes before getting in with him.

"Oh, hey baby, boy this car so nice, I would of got in without knowing who you was." She said with a smirk.

"Whatsup ma, you alright?"

"Hell naw I ain't alright!" Renee shouts as if Rome wasn't sitting right next to her. "This motherfucker think he Don Corleone or some fucking body. Talking to me like I ain't shit. All the fucking money I done made his ass, I got people coming from Taylor to holla at his ass. Ungrateful bitch!!! I swear I should of stopped dealing with his ass when he got my son killed. I don't know what the hell I was ….."

"Hold on, hold on what?" Rome interrupted. "What you just say?"

"Uh, what?" Renee played the dumb role as if she didn't just lay the bait.

"Ma, what you just say, you said when he got your son killed. What that suppose to mean?"

Renee looked at him like he had two noses or something. "What you think it mean Rome? C'mon now Rome wakeup and smell the coffee, that nigga was behind that shit. The whole hood know it, he ain't lost a bit of sleep since that shit happened. Who else you

164

know little cousin get killed, then 2 weeks later he open up and start selling dope out the same exact apartment. Plus, Jake got killed with a Police issued 40-cal glock. You know Omar stepdad work for the 10th precinct and he be buying them guns for him."

"But that don't make sense, why would he want Jake killed though ma?"

"Rome is you that naïve? Omar not only crazy and dumb, but he be power tripping. Jake was trying to do his own thing and sometimes he would bring his own work he bought from someone else and sell it in the spot, they loved Jake around here."

Rome could remember one instance when Jake copped some work from Ski and took it to Omar's spot. He damn near tripled his money and was all smiles the whole day, he said the fiends were saying it was the best they had in a long time. Don and Rome advised him not to make it a habit, but they never stayed on top of it.

"But ma, how you know all this, you wasn't even around like that?"

"Boy I been doing my homework, you don't think this shit eat me up. Look at me Rome!" Renee eyes start to water. "I loved my baby, I don't care what nobody say, that nigga gone get his! My baby was up and coming, shit he would have been right here riding with you, in a nice car just like yours." The last statement she made, hit Rome close to home and she knew it would, that was the icing on the cake.

"You can pull over right here, across the street from this gas station. I'm going right over there."

165

"Ma, you gone be alright, you need something? Hold up here." Rome pulled out a goatchoker and handed Renee three hundred dollar bills. "Get cleaned up ma, I don't like seeing you like this."

"I know baby, I'm a get it together."

"You still got my number right?" Rome asked.

"Huh huh, the 407 right?"

"Yeah call me if you need something, don't worry about that nigga, I'm a take care of it."

After dropping her off, Rome stayed in the vicinity, he circled the neighborhood silently waiting for Omar to pop back up. Rome didn't want another minute to pass without confronting this dude. After about twenty minutes passed, he witnessed Renee speed walking leaving the direction of Omar's spot, it was obvious she'd just copped with the money he just gave her. He shook his head and kept driving. Omar stood on the porch in a white tee smoking a Newport. It was around midnight, the block was quiet and Rome wanted to seize the opportunity. He made a quick u-turn, Omar took two steps back as he noticed this and flicked the cigarette. Natural instinct led him to reach for a pistol that wasn't there, but once he saw Rome get out the car, he relaxed.

"What's the deal playboy?" Omar spoke.

"Ain't nothing, what's going on?"

"You know, nothing major, making sure the operation run smooth, watching these little niggas. Just cause a nigga touching a little something don't mean my presence don't have to be felt."

"So whatsup, ain't nothing else surface on that situation?" Rome asked not really interested in the small talk. The temperature was high, you could feel the tension in the air. The baby 3-80 was burning a hole in Rome's pocket as Omar looked him dead in the eye.

"Dog you coming around here checking up on me, like you somebody I gotta answer to about my little cousin. I'm starting to think you got something you wanna get off your chest or something." His tone was harsh and attitude was evident as he walked towards Rome. Omar's voice had escalated, which is the reason why Tory was posted at the screen door. His hands weren't in clear view, Rome took notice and at that instant made his mind up.

"Bloch ah, Bloc Bloc!!" He gave Omar three face shots close range, he fell to the pavement with half his face blown off. Tory let off three shots wildly, more out of fear than anything, all from behind the screen door. Rome banged till his clip was empty, missing his second target as he slumped in his Audi, which was now short two windows.

"Arrrrhhh Arrhh!!" Tires screech as he pulls off, pistol on his lap as he drove with his left hand and cleaned the gun off using his t-shirt with his right. He wouldn't feel the burning sensation in his shoulder or the reality of what he'd done until his adrenaline wore off.

Chapter 22

Rome: "Damn dog straight up.., that's how you feel my nigga? You got me murking shit and everything huh? You out of order, fuck what you trying to get me the chair?"

Rio: (Rio sits silent)

Rome: "Oh you don't hear me now? What, cat got your tongue?"

Rio: "For the umpteenth time man, I wish you just let me do my job, I had a nice little flow going."

Rome: "Yeah I can't front this shit is starting to pick up. We might push some units after all." (Rome smiles)

Rio: "I told you just let me do me, follow my lead, I'll take you to the top."

Rome: "Holdup; pump ya brakes cuzzo, don't start feeling yourself. I respect the game though, so I'm a lay off for now."

Rio: "Bout time!"

****

It was December 28, 2003 and Don had exactly one year six months left to his out date. June 2005, what better time to touch down than the beginning of summer. Or in Don's mind his summer, like most prisoners he had replayed his release date over and over in his head. Minor details my change, but for the most part, his mission remained. The game wasn't out of his system yet, no need in him trying to fool himself otherwise. He still had a thirst for street fame. Don layed on his back in his bunk looking towards the ceiling, his boots were laced up tight with his hand on his street knife. At this point, he wasn't even comfortable in his own cell. Don couldn't look at himself in the mirror until he retaliated. He had grown to be a man of principle, and if that meant jeopardizing his freedom, then fuck it. When you choose to live by the codes of the game, you're not exempt to them.

"You want some of these chips dog?" Don's cellmate Boogie asks him. Don shakes his head no without looking at him.

Boogie looks outside the gate down the tier, then turns around with a grin stating, "Damn dog you can chill Charlie ain't coming," with a subtle laugh. Don just sat there silent not finding shit funny looking at his celly as his laughing ceased. It was an uncomfortable silence for a minute or two, then Don just burst out laughing. Boogie stood stunned for a minute, then joined in the laughter. At this point the ice was broken and Don admired his boldness. They spent the rest of the night getting acquainted and trading war stories, a new alliance was formed.

"DJ, hold up hold up, one second stop the music. Ladies and gentlemen let me have your attention for a second, just one second people, I know yall wanna get back to partying. This muthafucka packed tonight too! Damn! But we need to have a moment of silence for our fallen comrades. We lost two fellow Hell-Bounders this

169

past month and despite that, yall know the drill, this is a weekly routine."

The inner city and outskirts of Detroit were filled with motorcycle clubs, which some looked at as a sophisticated word for gang. Memberships varied from policeman, politicians to dopeman, prostitutes and strippers. The Hell-Bounders ran their operation with an iron fist, the pro-black motorcycle club could be spotted on the freeway in their embroidered black leather vests up to 30 deep any given day. Every Friday and Saturday night they held parties at their warehouse on E. Charlevoix after hours. The whole hood was in the building, Black Bottom especially. Hell-Bounders roamed the crowded warehouse making sure no outsiders touched their women or violated the rules. Caressing, dancing with or fraternizing with a female Hell-Bounder unwillingly could cost you. Consequences and repercussions consisted of death or being beat to a pulp. If you were interested in a woman wearing a Hell-Bounder's vest, you'd better think twice. You had no win in a warehouse with a one way exit, full of club members with guns and baseball bats.

"Alright that's more like it, good looking out yall," the club member spoke up through the microphone as he stood next to the DJ booth. "Hey Rhino! We got a hard headed one, this nigga don't know when to shutup!"

"Who? Where he at?" Rhino maneuvered through the crowd pointing, eyes moving frantically.

"Right there, dark-skinned with the blunt in his hand, this nigga still talking through our moment of

170

silence!!" The young kid looked around as if he was stuck on stupid.

"Whop!!" Rhino hit him so hard his feet lifted off the ground. The blunt flew in the air across the room.

"Clown ass nigga!" Rhino shouted as he smashed his face in with blow after blow. At 6'4 200 plus, Rhino didn't need backup, but that didn't stop his fellow Hell-Bounders from jumping in stomping him to a bloody mess. His entourage looked on, not daring to help.

"Alright that's more like it," the DJ spoke up as Rhino carried the young cat out on his shoulder and threw him outside the warehouse, the music was back on and it was back to business as usual.

"Damn girl wasn't that Shaniyah little brother, why you ain't stop that shit?" The bartender asked Dana.

"Shit that nigga know the rules, plus I just joined the club, I don't have no clout like that."

Dana was the newest addition to the Hell-Bounders Club. Black girl lost would be the appropriate term, she was at a point in her life where she was just doing whatever, going with the flow, living the party life. The length the Hell-Bounders would make women go through to join the club was always the talk of the town, though it was hard to separate fact from fiction. It was speculated that the women had to let the male members run trains on them to get initiated. Different tactics were used to make sure they could hold water,

171

and a boyfriend who wasn't affiliated, forget about it, no one was allowed to date outside the club.

"Girl never in a million years, would I have thought I'd be seeing you wearing that vest. I remember you use to come in here like, look at these bitches with them tired ass vests on praising these niggas." The bartender put her hands on her hips and screwed up her face imitating Dana.

"Girl I know, Rhino talked me into this shit. I'm only doing it for a minute, make me some money to put down on this house, then I'm out. Fuck all that till death do us part shit."

The bartender smiled, but she knew better, call her Sunshine Anderson, because she'd heard it all before. She watched Dana grow up and many others before her. She knew this was a way for Dana to supply her cocaine habit, while at the same time keeping it on the low, but that only last for so long. The bartender leans down towards Dana whispering in her ear.

"Dana, listen to me baby, I know you didn't have it easy coming up, but this not gone make it no better. Dana this ain't for you, why don't you just quit while you're ahead."

"Auntie, what you talking bout, I'm cool. Oh that's my song too," Dana says as she stands up grinding her hips. Snoop Dog's 'Beautiful' came through the speakers. Just then Rhino walked up and touched her behind.

"Grab it like you mean it baby, it's yours." Dana commented, then tongued him down before he

172

could respond.   Maxine the bartender, just shook her head and tended to her customers.

Chapter 23

You either ten toes in it or you not in it at all. Chuck's words rung in Rome's head as he contemplated on the latest events. Purple haze always put him deep in thought as thick clouds of smoke left his nostrils, Scarface's 'The Fix' album played in the background. In a rented Explorer with Ohio license plates, he sat waiting on Dre to pull up. Rome just left a meeting with Will (his connect) and it went sour, he was trying to cop a bird, but he only had $15,000. Will wouldn't let him owe him the $4,500, Rome even offered to give him an extra $3,000, but he wouldn't bulge. He stressed the fact that he didn't have it and needed cash on hand. Will claim things were tight right now, but Rome wasn't convinced, plus he knew the bag landed every 2nd week of the month and today was the 12th. Rome was forced to buy a half for $10,000 just so he could stay on. He'd been dealing with Will for 3 years, no shorts and always on time, and this was the thanks he got. "I should set his bitch ass up," Rome stated under his breath. After dishing out $20,000 for his workers funeral, cashing out the Audi for eighty, his spot in Black Bottom was the only one still standing and it had slowed up, but his spending habits and bills didn't. Add that to the fact that he was hot ass fish grease right now. Unnecessary heat from the murders of Omar, Butch and Corey had him paranoid and missing weight sales because he was trying to lay low. His right hand was in prison and he inherited his beef, 9x out of 10, money and beef don't mix and Charlie and Big T had the upper hand right now.

["Whoever said illegal was the easy way out, couldn't understand the mechanics, inner workings of the underworld granted."] Jay-Z never lied.

"Damn bout time nigga," Rome said to Dre as he pulled up in Black Bottom on Ellery St.

"What's the deal playboy?" Dre asked.

"Shit you know the deal, time to hit that highway. You holler at your cousin?"

"Yeah she waiting on you, everything in motion, she just said call her when you on your way."

"Ol boy been through your hood lately?" Rome asked, speaking of Big T.

"Yeah, I ran into that nigga at the Coney Island on Evergreen, spoke to him and shit, chopped it up with him like I ain't even know what happened. I can tell he was fishing though."

"You should of got at that nigga right there, you claim he don't never be slipping."

"Too many eyes was out there dog, I ain't no cowboy like you." Dre responded jokingly, talking bout how reckless Rome had killed Omar. "As long as his aunt live around the corner, one way or the other he can always get touched. Let's get this money back up first, then we can handle them niggas."

"Damn dog that's the first time you made sense in awhile." Rome said with a smirk.

Dre laughed before asking, "So what time you leaving?"

"In about a hour, I'm a let ol girl drive the bag down there and I'm a get on the greyhound. She say she

175

feel more comfortable driving, so fuck it. I'm a have Jamal ride with her, it's only a 4 ½ hour trip."

"You get on yet?"

"Yeah, I'm only gone take 9 (o's) down there to see how it's looking.'

"Nine?" Dre gave him a disapproving look. "That ain't enough."

"Dog it's my first trip down there."

"Man Chanel (Dre's cousin) gone laugh at you dog. That shit gone be gone in a couple hours."

"How you know, you ain't been down there in 2 years!"

"I'm telling you what I know dog, you good, what you need something?"

"Nah, I'm cool I'll at least take a half then." Dre still shook his head disagreeing. Eventhough through the past few years they'd built a tight bond, Rome still wasn't comfortable letting Dre know what he was working with or his every move. He loved Dre, but nevertheless the game had trained him that way.

"Hey switch whips with me right quick, I gotta take care of something before I leave."

"You would wanna switch with me while the Audi in the shop.'

"Shutup nigga, meet me back here in a couple hours." Rome jumped in Dre's 2004 bone white Lincoln

Mark LT pickup truck. Even at 6ft, the 26's made it sit up so high that he had to jump in.

Debra sat in the dining room with Carrie rubbing her fingers through her hair. "Oh girl your hair growing, its growing fast too.' Debra said looking at her daughter. Till this day, it amazed her how her children grew so fast. At 15, Carrie was starting to fill out and everything. She even had the nerve to have a slight attitude, not to mention she was conceited. Today she waited impatiently for her brother Rome to pick her up for an outfit / dress for her annual Christmas ball at the school.

"I wish he hurry up dang, I'm bout to call him." said Carrie standing up smacking her teeth.

"Girl sit down, he'll be here in a minute." Just then a horn honked outside. Debra hated it when someone did that. "I know that ain't him blowing no horn like he crazy." "Who is this in a cream truck?"

"Oh let me see, oh that's probably Rome in Dre truck. Carrie grabbed her coat and was out the door before Debra could protest or question anything.

Rome chopped the streets up in the Lincoln Mark LT as the hood waved and threw up the deuces. Coming from nothing, remembering days when the DOT bus was his only option, embarrassed to tell females where he lived let along let them in. Now with the couple dollars he was touching, and some nice whips at his disposal, Rome made sure he switched up cars on the constant. Not just to impress but naturally it was a habit he inherited from the game. Keep them guessing, male or female, friend or foe. All this came into play as the security lifted the gate while Rome pulled into the Jeffersonian Condominiums.

"Where we at Rome, the mall gone close," Carrie complained.

"Girl chill out, it's only 7:00, we got enough time." Rome responded as he pulled over and made a call. "I'm outside."

Five minutes later a chocolate voluptuous woman approached the truck with an aura that let you know she knew she was the shit.

Carrie gets out the truck, "Here you can get in the front."

"She ain't nobody, she could of sat in the back." Rome states jokingly.

His lady friend playfully hits him upside his head. "Boy be quiet, at least somebody got some manners."

Rome sat still in a daze as he was still stuck on the visual of her approaching the truck. I swear you would of thought Apple Bottoms were made specifically for her, but this evening she was draped in Baby Phat. Rome was feeling like Ginuwine, he was wondering how she got in those jeans. Tamara was the shit and she knew it. Her walk was mean like she was trained on the runway. Tamara's tall shapely figure could be credited to her high school basketball days, but when her father passed away she lost her passion for the game, became cold-hearted and quit the sport. Now, two kids and two years later with a gain of 20lbs., it was like icing on the cake to her already athletic build, 36c, 40 and 22in waist.

Tamara was spoiled rotten, so she was rebellious by nature, Charlie being a controlling baby father only added salt to the wound. "I would rather you be celibate, but if you do get a itch, just make sure I don't know the nigga, and it bet not be one of my homies or my enemies." She could recall Charlie telling her on numerous occasions. Yeah Rome was nice looking and she could tell he was bout a dollar, but going out with him was more of an adventure to her. She knew she was skating on thin ice, but the danger and spontaneity of it turned her on, plus she would have her cake and eat it too, Rome would definitely pay like he weigh.

Rome hit I-75 freeway on his way to Somerset Mall as he reflected back on the day he pulled Tamara........The Sweetwater Tavern had a full house that night and they caught each other looking at one another on more than one instant. Tamara sported a crispy wrap which brought out the youthful features in her face, wearing a Sean John one-piece catsuit. The few times she stood, she had every male in the restaurant's attention. Rome ran into her coming out the restroom, the second time she stood.

"Damn I love a woman that ride for her man." Rome said as she brushed pass.

"Well that would apply to me, if I had one," and with that she kept walking.

Back at her table 30-40 minutes later, the restaurant was near closing and the ladies were feeling good, all laughs and giggles.

179

"Bitch, you gone turn into a damn margarita, what you trying to prove ordering all that shit!!" One of the ladies said loudly to Tamara.

"Girl shutup, it ain't like you paying for it anyway. Charlie sent me two grand today, and I promised myself I would spend all of it recklessly. For leaving me...., (Tamara was buzzing, and her speech was slurred as she paused after every word she spoke.) out here ..., by myself with a wet pussy ...., a headache and these two rugrats." Tamara beated on the table for emphasis almost knocking the remaining dishes and drinks over.

Not knowing how to react, her girls grew silent for about 30 seconds. Ah ha ha!!! (laughter) Tamara burst out laughing, and they followed suit. "Waiter!!! (Tamara screams) Waiter we need our check!" The waiter arrives, an older man in his mid-forties.

"Yes miss, what is it?"

"We need our bill please."

"Oh ma'am its already taken care of along with my tip.'

"By who, are you sure?" Tamara asked eyebrows raised.

"The young man um, he left about 15-20 minutes ago, had on a black designer pea coat and scarf, black designer boots. "I know, Prada." (Tamara interrupts) "Huh?" he says before continuing. "He told me to give you this." Tamara looked at him funny as he handed her one of the establishment's job applications.

180

"What the…..," she was reluctant to take it, then snatched the paper. Her uneasiness turned into a smile as she read: "I would love to apply for the position," written in large letters. Next to the name, it read, Rome along with his number next to the phone. Corny, but cute she thought, plus the $700 tab he picked up wasn't bad either.

Two weeks later, Tamara was still playing hard to get, but giving Rome enough hints for him to keep pushing. "You alright?" she asked Rome as he found a spot in the mall parking lot.

"Yeah I'm cool, I was just thinking about something."

"About what?"

"I can't get into all that right now, its kids in the car."

"Boy shutup," Tamara said giving him a playful nudge.

The threesome made their way through the mall all smiles, come to find out Carrie and Tamara were peas in a pod. Tamara a shopaholic and Carrie a shopaholic in training. Carrie stood in the mirror getting fitted for a Versace gown.

"You didn't tell me you had a daughter?"

"Are you serious, how old do you think I am?" Rome stated in shock. "That's my little sister, she my heart, I don't have any kids."

"Oh." That caught Tamara by surprise and gave her a newfound respect for Rome especially her being a sibling herself. The saleswoman rung up Carrie's items and they made their way to the exit looking like they robbed the joint. Shopping must have been an aphrodisiac for Tamara because she turned into someone else during the ride home.

"Damn I like it when he stand up at attention on command." Tamara said while rubbing Rome's inner thigh as he drove. Her hands found their way from his thigh to the opening of his zipper, Rome was hard as a brick. "You like that daddy," she said as she slowly stroked his shaft up and down. Rome was turned on by the boldness of her actions with his little sister right in the backseat. He was driving like a bat out of hell trying to get her home.

"Oh, slow down before I make a mess." Rome said as he abruptly grabbed her wrist. Tamara seductively placed her index finder in her mouth, licking the pre-cum off the tip, using her finger to imitate her oral skills.

"Alright see you later, nice meeting you...," Carrie was cut off mid-sentence as Rome pulled off, she could barely get her bags out the truck. Before Rome made it off the block Tamara had him in her mouth. "Ohhhhh, Awww, shiiit!" She had Rome stuttering and frowning his face.

"You like that baby?" Tamara looked Rome in the eyes as she rubbed the head of his penis around her lips, then deep throated him. She took all of his 9 inches in with ease and Rome was on the verge of exploding.

182

"Damn you gone make me pull over. Ahhh!" ("Slurp, slurp…,") Tamara continued sucking and made a popping noise before stopping.

"I don't know what you waiting on?" she spoke up. With that said, Rome recklessly whipped the truck into a deserted street. Surprisingly, Tamara got out the truck so Rome followed suit, dick hard and all. Quickly Tamara slid her jeans down exposing her bare behind, she was pantyless and her camel toe stuck out as she bent over the passenger seat.

"Come get this pussy daddy," Tamara spoke seductively as she used her hands to spread her butt cheeks. Rome wasted no time as he gave her what she was asking for. Tamara tensed up taking the pain like a champ as she sucked her fingers to muffle the noises. Rome started out with slow long deep strokes. Teasingly inserting the head in and out of her pussy, Aquafina ain't have nothing on her.

"Ohh baby fuck me please….," Rome gripped her hips and started beating the pussy up like it stole something. "Ohhh Ah uh…., huh. (moans) uh. Oh my god….Oh."

"You like that?"

"Y-E-S!! Yeah…Ahh!!"

"I can't hear you!" Rome was pounding like he had something to prove.

"I'm bout to come baby…, Oh shit!!! Rome felt her tense up and her legs started to shake.

"I'm right behind you baby!!!" he shouted out.

183

"Oh, come with me baby, please!" Tamara reached back and tickled his balls, Rome arched her back and released himself inside her, marking his territory.

"Oh my god! Boy! I ain't never did nothing like this before." She said immediately afterwards as if she was oblivious to her surroundings. I hope ain't nobody see us!" They made their way back to Tamara's condo to finish what they started.

Chapter 24

"Yo, I'm telling you dog, this bitch suck my dick so good, I thought I had my feeling back for a minute. I'm making faces and shit, like I could actually feel that shit."

"Ah ha ha ha (laughter. Ay you a silly mothafucka." Rome was laughing his heart out as he listened to Ronnie Moe reflect on his escapade from last night.

"First stop!! Dayton, Ohio!!" The greyhound bus driver shouts through the loud speaker.

"Look man, I'm a hit you when I touch, we at the first stop I'm bout to get off and charge this phone." Rome steps off the bus eyes wide scanning his surroundings, eventhough the work was on the freeway with his driver Kameesha, he still was paranoid. He plugged up the phone and called Dre's cousin Chanel.

Andrea stood in the refreshment line watching Rome during his entire conversation. Her first thought was to dodge him until his bus loaded back up, but she quickly fought off the idea. Something about this young guy had her curious, she just couldn't put her hands on it at the moment. Andrea checked her lip gloss and braced herself, at the angle Rome was standing he was sure to notice her.

Rome: "As if I wasn't already distracted and had enough on my mind, I spot her in line for a soda. I swear it seem like she ain't have no flaws."

Rio: "Come on now, no flaws?"

185

Rome: "I bullshit you not dog, or unless she had me so open I didn't wanna see any. I remember thinking like damn, everything happen for a reason, I wasn't even gone fuck with the bus. Yall know I had to step to her right? Even with her back turned, I had the feeling like she had peeped me first, it's like I felt her energy."

Rio: "Come on man, you cut in like you was gone give us some real details."

Rome: "Alright, alright chill. Can you believe she act like she ain't know who I was. I tapped her and she turned around gripping her coach bag."

"Do I know you?" Andrea asks with agitation in her voice.

"Girl quit playing with me."

"Excuse me?" Andrea's expression was stern. Rome was dumb-founded, then suddenly she broke the ice with a smile and a subtle laugh.

"You the last person I expected to see on the Greyhound."

"And why is that?"

"I just didn't have you as the greyhound type."

"Well I wish you tell me what type I am because every time you see me, I'm a different type." Andrea says as she reaches in her purse to pay for her refreshments. Rome stops her and picks up the bill. Andrea gives him a look as if to say, "Wow," but appreciates the gesture. They move on to the sitting area.

186

"I don't know you just seem too high maintenance to catch the Greyhound. Look at you, you the only one in here with three inch heels on." This made Andrea laugh.

"No I'm not high-maintenance, I just like nice things, it's a difference."

"Oh I see, treat yourself don't cheat yourself." Andrea smiles again, her light caramel skin is home to two deep dimples. Her dark brown eyes are welcoming, and the thin strand of hair that kept blocking her eye added to her sex appeal.

"See what I tell you about staring."

"Whatever, so what you doing around these parts?"

"Nosy?" Now it was Rome's turn to laugh. "I'm on vacation visiting family for the weekend, what about you?"

"Same here."

"Hmmm. You answered to fast, I don't believe you."

"Damn you don't trust me already?"

"A women's intuition, what's your name and how old are you?"

"Slow down." Andrea smiles. The two sat and got acquainted for the remainder of the layover. Surprisingly, Andrea had been out the loop for two years, a few dates off and on nothing serious. Rome asked about her past relationships, but she became defensive so he let it go. It was a seven year age difference, Rome 21, she 28, but neither seemed to care. The chemistry was evident, although Andrea teasingly called him a baby throughout the evening. It became awkward when it was time to part ways.

Rome stood so close to Andrea he could feel her breath, as she waits at the gate while her bus loads, both of them nervous, neither knowing what to say.

"So I guess I'll call you this weekend."

"Yeah you said that already." Rome smiles, he can't recall ever being this excited to see someone again. Their eyes lock as she boards the bus, he scans her figure one last time before the door closes.

****

Meanwhile on Burt Rd in Brightmoor, Dre sits on his grandma's block with his seat back, feet on the dash. On the phone with his new lady friend, he fails to notice the dark tinted Aerostar van that circles the block for the third time. At 1:30 in the afternoon, on a Saturday, kids crowd the block playing double dutch and two square. Sometimes Dre would just park here and talk shit all day and might even fall asleep in the truck, that's how comfortable he feels. This is his home turf, where he sold his first rock, got his first piece of pussy. He closes his phone shut and grabs the handle to open the door when all of a sudden, shots rang out simultaneously. "Tat tat att tat tat, bloc ah bloc ah bloc ah..." Dre curls up under the steering wheel for cover. Two men let off rounds through the sliding doors of the van. One of them unleashes an AK47 with a hundred round drum resembling Rambo. Kids scramble and scream as the gunfire seems like it lasts for eternity. When it finally ceased, the block is stunned, and everyone is afraid of the outcome. Smoke fills the air and his truck is riddled with bullet holes. Down the block, Dre's aunt stands on the porch in a state of shock with her hand covering her mouth. She takes baby steps towards the truck while everyone watches, fearing her worst nightmare may become a reality.

Dana is damn near doing ninety on the Edsel Ford Freeway. She called herself doing a good deed by taking her grandmother shopping, but it turned into a disaster. All her life it's like her grandmother looks past the good and can only find the negative in any situation. It's like in her eyes she couldn't do right, anything less than a saint was unacceptable. While walking out of Marshall Fields in Eastland Mall, Dana ran into two Hell-Bounders, wearing their leather vests and boots looking like bonafied hoodlums. As soon as they noticed her, they addressed her by her club name disregarding her grandmother.

"Ladybug, whatsup?" Dana tried to keep walking as if she didn't hear them.

"Ladybug, why you ain't representing?" they asked referring to her not wearing her vest.

"Are those people talking to you?" Ms. Wiles asks. Dana has no choice but to acknowledge the two as they approach them looking intimidating.

"Whatsup baby, why you acting like you don't know nobody, and where your vest at? How you doing miss?" he speaks to Ms. Wiles before he continues.

189

Dana hugs both of them while Ms. Wiles stands there furious and in shock. She grew up in the neighborhood and she's aware of what the Hell-Bounders are about. She's infuriated that Dana would even associate with their kind. To make matters worse, the bulkiest dude of the two hugs Dana and grips her ass like he owns it, then taps it twice before letting go. This even catches Dana off guard, fast forward thirty minutes later, her grandmother hasn't stopped yelling yet.

"Lord, lord, where did I go wrong? I should of sent your ass down south with your auntie, and I hope you don't think I'm keeping none of this. There's no telling what you did to get the money for it."

"Grandma I don't even care no more!" Dana was fed up.

"You don't care, you don't care? I'm not surprised you don't even care about yourself, ain't nothing but a slut just like your mother!" "Arrggh.., arrrgh," the car comes to a halt.

Dana yells, "Get the hell out of my car, now! You don't have no right to talk about my mother like that!" Its broad day and they have the whole block attention, this catches Ms. Wiles off guard, Dana has never stood up to her. She sits there with a stern look staring into her eyes. "Enough is enough damnit! I try I swear, I try, ain't shit ever good enough for you." Dana is angry and broken, a few tears roll down her cheek, more out of anger than sadness. Her grandmother steps out the car.

"I don't ever wanna see your ass at this house again When them streets chew you up and spit you out,

190

don't come running back to me. You think them men love you, your ass gone learn." She snatches the earrings out her ear that Dana just bought for her and tosses them in the car, then slams the door.

Chapter 25

Meanwhile at Ryan Correctional Facility

Charlie sits on his bunk tapping his feet with his fists balled up. His cellmate entered the cell, noticed how mad he was and turned back around. He sweats from shadow boxing, in an attempt to calm his nerves and ease his aggression. Usually mail call is the best time of the day for him, he gets heavy mail on the daily basis. Today was different as he sat on his bunk looking at the photographs for the umpteenth time. Tamara lay in the bed next to a man with his face blurred out, each picture showing her in various sexual positions on the receiving end. One photo show Tamara on her knees displaying her deep throat skills, as if that wasn't enough the last photo shows Tamara and the dude laid in the bed with his son in the middle sleep. Inside the envelope a note reads: "You sure you wanna play this game?" Charlie has an idea of who could be behind this, but his pride won't let him believe it. When he called Tamara she swore up and down it wasn't her, she begged him to mail her the pictures, but he refused. She claimed anything could be done with today's technology, but being with her for 10 years he knew better. Charlie knew her body, her condo and the tattoo on the small of her back gave her away. The tables were turned, these cats knew where his son laid his head. Charlie hurriedly called Big T to cancel his next move.

"Ay yo, that surprise I told you to give ol boy, cancel that."

"It's too late, he already got it. What's the deal?"

"Fuck!! Nothing man, shit crazy, I need you to come up here and see me A.S.A.P."

****

Columbus, Ohio, home to roughly 700,000 had history with Detroit. Back in the late eighties a swarm of Detroiters flooded the city trying to seize the drug trade, they ended up going to war with some boys from Gary, Indiana who were on the same mission. Bodies piled up and the city was turned upside down, it would later be know as the "trench coat mafia." So when Rome touched down he was treated like royalty on the strength of his hometown. Right now he was meeting Chanel on the northside near OSU campus, she pulled up in a BMW X5, feeling herself blasting Crime Mob 'Knuck if you Buck.' Rome became irritated as he noticed a man riding with her in the passenger seat, this was his 4th trip down here and it seemed she was getting too comfortable. He made a mental note to address her about bringing unfamiliar faces around. Dre was right, Chanel basically laughed at him when she realized he'd only bought a half a bird with him. Not literally, but she let it be known that it was elementary to her.

"Shit you might as well not even unpack your stuff, I can get rid of that right now," were her exact words as she searched through her phone dealing #'s. "What, that's all you had?"

"Naw, you know I just wanted to test the waters first it ain't nothing if you gotta sale for it, it can go." Rome stated knowing he really wanted to break it down.

"Alright, I can get you $13,500 for it now, we out," she said calling Rome's bluff.

193

Now a week and a half later, he was on his fourth trip to Columbus, but Chanel thought it was his second. After he sold the first half to Chanel's boy Chico, he cut out the middleman and dealt with Chico on his own for two trips. Chico had crazy clientele, he had a bunch of dudes buying bigs (4 ½ oz's) and ounces (all hard) like it was nickel rocks at a $1,000 a pop. All Chico wanted was his work at a lower price and for Rome to front him whatever he buy.

Rome: "No, no, no, you got it twisted. Man you always make the hustle sound messed up. Look, as I learned a long time ago, looking like money, can make you money. You never let the clio (clientele) know how long your reach is, if you only got a ounce, play it like you got 4 ½. If you only working with a chirp, play it like you holding 2 or 3 chirps."

Rio: "What the hell is a chirp?"

Rome: "Figure it out stupid, quit cutting me off. But yeah that way you keep the clio on your line and if they call your bluff and try to cop heavy, you middleman and still make you a couple dollars. But that's not the key, the main thing is you keeping them around for when you do get your weight back up, they still on your line copping from you. See I couldn't let Chanel know I was fucked up, I had to sell the illusion that I had whatever she needed, but at the same time I needed the town to come up. I wanted to keep my fronts up, so that next night I cut into Chico, he was cautious at first, but I hit him with the lingo and willed him in. I utilized my plugs and came back with a chirp and a half. Sold him the half for 10 all shine, I didn't even hit it. (cut it) I ended up bringing the chirp back to about 51 ounces. I offed it in 2 days at 950 a pop and got on the highway

194

with 60 (grand) plus 10 from him because I told him I needed it to cop with. I was officially back, I had found a goldmine.

Rio: "Rome I could of made all that sound a lot more interesting. This is a novel not a conversation."

Rome: "Man I really live this shit, whatever I say, gone sound interesting."

****

Rome contemplated on the past few weeks as he rode in the backseat of Chanel's X5. He'd been going super hard lately, on some renegade shit, all he did was cop, play the highway, cop and play the highway again. He put his social life on the backburner, not purposely but the flip had him open. He hadn't talked to Dre, or got at Don either. The flip wasn't the only thing that had him open though, him and Andrea had spent numerous nights talking on the phone for hours like teenagers. It didn't take long for him to realize she was a different breed. Their first date was to hear spoken word at The Music Hall, she already had him experiencing new things. As of now, they were checking in at least every other night. Columbus was bringing Rome that scary money, money was coming so fast, it would scare you. In just a week, he turned a half of bird into four. With 80 grand and some change to his name, Rome said fuck it and went for the gusto. He copped four birds for $75,000, Chanel had been pressing him to make sure he be ready, she had some white boys coming from Lexington, Kentucky who were willing to pay $35,000 a bird as long as it was still in the wrap. It was drought season down there and they were desperate. All Rome wanted was 30, he told Chanel she could keep the 5 off

195

each one. He'd still score a clean $45,000 profit, his palms were sweating thinking about it from excitement, this would be the biggest score of his career.

"So, where you know this dude from?" Rome asked Chanel after her company exited the car.

"Oh he ain't nobody, just a nigga I keep on standby to handle my bills and shit, he like to be controlled." Chanel says arrogantly. Chanel resembled a thicker version of Monica Calhoun and her attitude was similar to her character in the movie "The Players Club." Typical good girl, gone bad, now she was gone forever. She sold her soul for the love of designer brands, fast money and fast cars.

"I ain't talking about him, I'm talking about these white boys we about to meet."

"Oh, Tommy Lee and Jesse, they harmless, I met them when I used to go to Ohio State. They come from money, they just wanna be down and swear they black. You don't have nothing to worry about, wait until you see them, you gone be cracking up."

"Where we meeting them at again?"

"Tommy Lee own a loft downtown, his father bought it for him while he was in school before he went back home."

Five minutes later, Chanel pulls up to the lofts and parks on a side street. The streets are bustling with traffic due to rush hour, at 5 p.m. people are just leaving work. Chanel gets out the X5, turns back and looks at Rome shockingly as he remains in the front seat hesitant. "You cool? I'll go in and handle it if you want me to."

196

Chanel is anxious to score a quick $20,000 free and clear. The whole ride there she thought about what she's going to do with the money. Rome grabs the duffel bag out the backseat, as much as he'd rather make the sale in third person, his gut won't let him trust Chanel with $140,000. He doesn't know if there's anybody waiting in that loft, or if Tommy Lee and Jesse even exist. More importantly, he wanna make sure the money is right and everything else is secure.

"I'm a leave the work in here, let's make sure everything cool first."

"Boy you stay paranoid, come on." Chanel says impatiently as they cross the street towards the loft. Rome scans his surroundings out of habit, no one is paying him attention, but he feels like all eyes are on him. The building is brick, four stories high, with two lofts on each floor. As soon as you enter the lobby, it's like you could smell the money bouncing off the walls. They were adorned with expensive paintings, and the desk are of the finest pine wood. They enter the loft confronted by a weed aroma and the sounds of TI's hit 'Rubber Band Man.' A skinny white boy with a goatee opens the door wearing an oversized Rocawear denim jean set with 6 in timberlands. His platinum Cuban link hangs to his belly button.

"Chanel baby, what it do?" He greets Chanel with a hug then looks towards Rome. "This must be the man of the hour right here. Whatsup homie?" He reaches out to give Rome some dap while introducing himself as Tommy Lee. Rome is amused inside at how hard this dude is trying.

"Boy sit your ass down, what I tell you about getting high off your own supply." (laughter fills the background)

"Chanel I see you still got jokes, and you still the same, always straight to business." Tommy Lee says as he sits a duffle bag on the table next to a money counting machine. He places the money in the machine $10,000 at a time.

"Tommy Lee where Jesse at?"

"Oh he up in Aspen, left the workload on me as usual." Chanel exits informing Tommy Lee that she'll be right back with his product.

Meanwhile Rome stands beside the window looking downwards at the downtown traffic until the noise of the money counting machine stops, snapping him out of his daze.

"There you go, $140,000," Tommy Lee breaks the uncomfortable silence. "So how's the product?" he asks Chanel as she returns with the four birds.

"A-1 still in the wrap, you won't be disappointed."

"Man that's music to my ears, I'll be ready again in a week or two, but we gotta talk about that number, it's too high."

"We can work something out, but I gotta holla at my peoples first." Rome is ready to get out of dodge, he can go without the small talk. Chanel cuts off the conversation as if she was reading his mind.

"Rome the money straight?"

"Yup," Rome answers as he stands walking towards the duffle bag full of cash.

"Hold on, let me crack a few of them open first," Tommy Lee says retrieving a switchblade from his pocket slicing through the duct tape. This is all new to Chanel, as soon as she opens her mouth to protest, the door of the loft is kicked in almost knocking it off the hinges. "FREEZE!!! FBI! GET DOWN!! DOWN NOW!!" Four agents rush the loft with guns drawn tackling Chanel to the ground first. Rome instantly backpedals towards the window with his 40-cal drawn, aimed and ready to shoot. He's not going out without a fight, fuck sitting in a courtroom facing football numbers.

Chapter 26

Ryan Corrections

"I don't know how it happened, but I'm sure what I saw. What the fuck nigga, you think I don't know my own family!" Charlie shouts with his face bent up.

Big T sat at the other end of the table in the visiting room watching his right hand lose his cool for the first time since they were kids. "Calm down man you making a scene."

"I'm saying nigga, you sitting here second guessing me like I'm a clown or something. I swear if that bitch wasn't the mother of my son, I would have been put her in the dirt. She sat right here and listened to me speak on the situation."

"You sure it was Rome and them? I figured they a stay in they place after the message we sent. Ain't shit moving over there on Burt Rd., they not making a penny. So what you trying to do?" Big T asked not really looking for an answer. "Lil Ronnie and them already got at Dre, so we might as well send Tamara and the kids up to the cabin in Mt. Pleasant, then we can strap up and go to war."

Charlie sat rubbing his chin deep in thought. "I know one thing, it ain't gone be no war, more like a massacre, them niggas reach ain't long enough. Just sit back for a minute, let me think on it, pack Tamara and the kids and take them to Mt. Pleasant, I'll get back with you in a couple days."

Back in Columbus

"Just put the gun down son, we can work something out, you still got your whole life ahead of you." The only black federal agent in the loft tries to plead with Rome. Rome notices Tommy Lee isn't cuffed and aims the gun in his direction.

"Motherfucker you set us up, I should of known!" Chanel lays pinned to the floor with her face mushed in the carpet, the feds show her no mercy. Tommy Lee stands there dumbfounded, his silence confirming his guilt.

"Son listen to me, don't turn this into something ugly. Stand clear guys," he tells his partners as he walks toward Rome with his gun lowered motioning for his team to be cool. Rome backs up and aims his 40-cal back towards the agent. The agent stops and his backup draws their weapons.

"Stop!!! I swear back the hell up or I'll let this motherfucker blow!" Rome backpedals faster, checks his back one last time and jumps through the glass window, shocking his onlookers. The agent runs to the window ready to shoot, but he's afraid he may hit an innocent bystander from 2 stories high. "Move out now!! He's heading south on High St."

Rome thinks his ankle is broken, if it isn't it feels like it, he heard two crackling sounds as he landed, but his adrenaline won't allow him to feel any pain right now. He resembles a bankrobber as he runs for dear life with his gun visible in broad daylight. He approaches an intersection and encounters a 20-something year old black woman with her son.

"Mommy he got a gun! Mommy look!!" The little boy points as his mom notices Rome at her window with gun in hand.

"Let me in I got money!!" Rome shouts as he beats on the window in the middle of traffic, wad of money in left hand, gun in his right. Before the woman can protest or lock the doors, he lets himself in through the back door. "Drive!" he shouts as he tosses the wad of money in her lap. Rome look deranged, his clothes are disheveled, and his face is bleeding due to the cuts he suffered from jumping through the window. The woman sits there shell shocked, horns blare behind her. "Go! I'm not gone hurt you, someone is after me!" She pulls off recklessly and scared.

"Man fuck that bitch, it's part of the game, it is what it is…, Bloc Ah Bloc Ah!!" Dana tosses and turns before jumping up in a cold sweat. Almost seven years later and Odell's words and the two shots that sealed his fate still haunted her and gave her nightmares. To her left Rhino snores heavily as he sleeps like a baby. Dana gets out the bed, grabs her cigarette case out of her panty drawer and goes straight to the bathroom. She opens the case retrieving a miniature straw and goes right to work, tilting her head taking one long toot. Her inability to face her fears and deal with life's harsh realities led her here. Dana looks in the mirror disappointed at what she sees, her habit has gotten worse and it's starting to show. She need cocaine to start her day, end it, and in the middle of the night to deal with these nightmares. Here nose was starting to swell and her face was losing its color.

"Fuck!" She murmurs as she attempts to do another line and notice she's on E. "Shit!" Dana dances around the bathroom before a lightbulb goes off in her head. She tiptoes back to the bedroom attempting to be discreet but Rhino awakens just as she retrieves the ounce of cocaine he was suppose to sell earlier that day. Dana flinches upon being noticed.

"Baby I was only gone take a little, I needed it, I been having them nightmares again." Dana says red-handed with the puppy dog face. Rhino's stare could burn a hole through her chest. She knows this look all too well.

"Bitch you sound like a real junkie you know that. Nightmare or not, your ass would have been tweaking."

Dana's face quickly forms into a menacing frown. How dare this old ass has been talk to her this way, is the thought that crosses her mind. With all her might Dana throws the ounce of cocaine and strikes Rhino smack dead in the face, the powder scatters across the room.

"Stupid bitch!!" Rhino dives towards Dana missing her as he stumbles and she dashes towards the bathroom. "Get your dumb ass over here," Rhino snatches her up by the hair, tossing her to the ground. She's a ragdoll compared to Rhino's monstrous frame, but nevertheless Dana is putting up a fight. She kicks her legs and swings her arms wildly as Rhino drags her back to the living room by her hair. "I don't know who the fuck you think you dealing with. Smack!! Smack!!" Rhino grips her by the throat backhanding her until she lost every bit of fight in her.

203

"Ahhh!! (screaming) Dana screams and wepts loudly.

"Turn your ass around, I know what you want." Rhino is trying to turn her over on her stomach.

"No! Get off of me!!" Dana yells and beats on his chest attempting to put up a fight again. Rhino eventually flips her over and rips off her satin panties, she continues to squirm and tries her best to protest.

"Be still bitch, you know you want it, fucking junkie slut." Rhino pulls out and shoves his whole ten inches inside her asshole forcing himself on her.

"Ahh!! Ahhh!" Dana screams in pain as her insides get tore open. Rhino has all his weight on her, giving her all he's got. The blood and screams only excites him, it's like he's turned into someone else.

"Uh hum, you know you like it," he has Dana back arched and pent down with his forearm. Her neck is twisted mashed into the carpet as he penetrates. Tears of pain and agony storm down Dana's face, she wants to scream, but her voice is gone. She blinks out before Rhino ejaculates.

Balloons and flowers fill the hospital room, the only sounds come from the machine signaling life. Rome stands looking on as his partner in crime lay in coma. "I should of listened to you dog," he says to Dre as if he's going to respond. Dre told him to chill until they got they're cash up, but he let his ego get the best of him and he just had to send the pictures. Rome feels like all this could have been avoided, little did he know the plan was already in motion.

"He fell into a coma right after the surgery. Good thing witnesses were close by and they responded fast. The chest wounds were severe and one grazed his head. The bullet wounds in his lower back and forearm along with the graze confirms he was ducking and slouched over during the gunfire."

"So what, do you think he'll make it?" Rome asks impatiently interrupting the doctor.

"Hmm." The doctor exhales and tilts his head. "Well the surgery went well, but with nine wounds from a AK47, he lost a lot of blood especially from the neck wound. I say its 60/40 but he may suffer memory loss or possibly be paralyzed if he does survive."

Rome nods.

"I'm gonna give you some time alone for a second, visiting is almost over."

"Listen doc." Rome grips his forearm and stops him in his tracks. He pulls out a wad of money, about $3,500 in 20's, 50's and 100's. "Man here take this," he attempts to slide the money inside the pocket of his lab coat. "This is just to show my appreciation.

"I'm sorry I can't take this," the doctor tries to give it back as the nurse looks on in the doorway.

"Look take it, I need my man to live, it's just a tip." Rome grips his back arm tighter, the doctor lets the money drop to the floor and storms out the room. Rome stands there trying to mask his sobbing. The nurse observes for a few more minutes before walking in. The past two hours, she's been trying to figure out why Rome looks so familiar, then it hits her. Tia gasps and covers her mouth with her hand, and matches Rome's face with the young boy she spotted the day she was with Ski. Lately, he had been all Andrea seems to talk about, how cute he was, or how his maturity shocked her at his age.

"You alright?" Rome asked breaking her out of her trance. He notice Tia standing there as if she just received some devastating news.

"Yeah I'm cool, the question is are you alright?"

"Well you know, could be better, you gone be the one helping to look after my boy?"

"Yes, more than likely, I give these people 12 hours a day."

"Here take care of him." Rome hands Tia the wad of money, and makes his way out before she could protest. Tia flips her phone to call Andrea, "Girl you not gone believe who just left out of here, meet me up here on my break."

****

Ryan Corrections

Leave it up to Rome, he would send the pictures, it would break Charlie's spirit and the beef would settle. Yeah well, Don was right here in the midst of it, and he knew better. Rome did what he could to persuade Don let it be until he was released, but right now Rome couldn't relate, his pride wasn't on the line and he

206

wasn't walking around everyday with his manhood in question. In order for things to go smooth, Don had to make his move swift and quick. After three weeks of strategizing and spreading some paper around, him and Boogie had their plan in motion. Don had been curled up in the laundry cart for the past 45 minutes hidden under some state blues and laundry bags. He checked his watch for the fourth time while gripping the street knife in his sweaty right palm. "About five more minutes," he says to himself.

"Tap, tap." Don positions himself in the laundry cart as the two taps is his signal that Charlie was on his way to the laundry room. Every 2nd week of the month Charlie used his laundry job to drop off his packages to each block. C-block was his last stop, and leave it up to Don, it would be his last stop literally. The door shuts, and as Charlie walks in Don gets in a squatted position under the clothes ready to spring up like 'jack in the box.' Charlie shuts the dryer off and reaches to retrieve the lint trap, the stash spot for his package. Don springs up out the laundry cart, the element of surprise has Charlie stuck, his eyes bulging is his only defense reaction. "Bitch ass nigga!!" "Ahh, ahh!" (screams) The first blow strikes Charlie in the neck, Don covers Charlie's mouth with his hand to muffle the sounds as he strikes him once more in the neck finishing off with two more blows to the stomach. Blood was everywhere as Charlie slides to the floor with his eyes wide. Don spits on him for emphasis, wipes the knife and washes his hands. He grabs his extra pair of state blues and changes, everything is right on schedule, yard is returning as he leaves and blends in with the crowd.

207

(One Week Later)

Don could hardly enjoy or concentrate on his phone call because of his paranoia. They had to ship Charlie out on the chopper, and he just knew any day, they would be coming for him, either his goons or the authorities. The feeling was in the air, shit was about to hit the fan.

"I swear this nigga got one more time to put his hand on me, baby I can't wait until you get out. I'm losing it, I'm sitting here wearing shades in my own damn house." Dana says as she removes her shades while looking in the mirror at the same time. "This shit is ridiculous." (laughter) Don chuckles on the other end. "Boy I know you not laughing, that shit ain't funny."

"I thought you said you got the locks changed?" he asks.

"This motherfucker don't give me no room to breathe to get the locks changed. Everytime I look up the nigga watching me like a hawk. Damn nigga give me some space." Dana was running the same ole game, yeah her situation was unfortunate, but its two sides to every story.

"You could leave if you wanted to, I ain't trying to hear that shit."

"Don I'm serious, you just don't know...."

"Shit, here these motherfuckers come!"

"Who? What you talking bout?"

"They on the block right now, call and tell Rome they got me." Six CO's enter the block in armor vests and shields like they were on their way to World War II.

"Folsom!! 45-1967, hang up the phone, you coming with us."

"I love you baby." Don got his last words out.

"Folsom hang up the phone now!!" The cornfed white boy out the bunch yelled and became aggressive with Don as he slapped the cuffs on him.

Chapter 27

That's what's crazy about the game, any given day you could lose it all. Just as fast as you get it, it could be gone even faster, it was a high stakes gamble. Once again Rome found himself right back at square one, he started second guessing himself like maybe he wasn't built. But those thoughts were quickly replaced with vengeance and a get back by any means mentality, fuck the rules nobody else followed them anyway.

After pulling a stakeout outside Tamara's condo for the past 6 hours, Rome & Ronnie Moe pulled off disappointed. It seemed Tamara was ten steps ahead of them, all her numbers were changed and the gate attendant said he hadn't seen her in a few weeks.

"You went at it the wrong way Rome, fuck them pictures and shit, you either gone send a message or you ain't, them niggas ain't playing with yall, so don't play with them. So what's next, what you gonna do?" Ronnie Moe asks from the passenger seat with a baby AK layed across his lap. Rome just nodded as he maneuvered through traffic. It was no debating, everything Ronnie Moe was saying made sense.

(phone rings) Rome checks the caller ID and tosses the phone back on the console frustrated.

"That's her again?" Ronnie Moe asks referring to Andrea. She'd been calling all day, but he'd been so caught up and distracted.

"Man gone head and holla at your lady, get this shit off your mind for a minute, but think about what I said. You got the deadliest nigga in a wheelchair on the

210

planet on your team, this shit is nothing." Ronnie Moe says as Rome helps him exit the car.

About a half hour later, he pulls up to Benihana's in Dearborn to meet Andrea. Rome spots her sitting near the window looking fresh off the red carpet. She stands and greets him with a hug, dressed in a cream Christian Dior pantsuit that fits her curves perfectly and Christian Loboutin hells. She's all smiles as Rome takes his seat.

"Long time no see stranger."

"What's going on, you miss me?" Rome asks rhetorically.

"Nah not really." Andrea responds and they both laugh.

After finishing they're entrees, Rome orders drinks, grey goose and cranberry for him, white zinfandel for her as they start to relax and open up. The conversation is flowing, but Andrea notices Rome is somewhere else, she wasn't getting his undivided attention and he wasn't his usual self.

"Baby what's wrong?" Andrea asks as she reaches her hand across the table placing it on top of his. Rome looks her in the eye and shakes his head indicating nothing is wrong. Andrea sighs, and sits back displaying attitude.

"I wish you stop playing and let me in, I got eyes, I can see Rome."

"What's that supposed to mean?"

"Boy first of all, I know you don't do know landscaping, who you think you fooling? Plus Tia told me she saw you at the hospital earlier and you gave her $3,500. So you know what, why don't we start over, because it was some things I wasn't too honest with you about either." Rome is appalled, but doesn't reveal it, he lets her continue. "When I ran into you at the greyhound station, I wasn't really visiting family." Andrea pauses before continuing. "My ex-husband has been incarcerated in a federal prison for the past 5 years and I was on my way to visit him. He's pressed me to move on time and time again, but I've been celibate since he left, by choice. We're not together, but I refuse to leave him in times of despair, plus he was so good to me, I feel obligated. You remind me so much of him, not in a bad, but in a good way, (Andrea smiles) but yet you're so different and new. When we talk, I feel a spark and you've awakened emotions in me I've had buried for so long. I want this to go somewhere, I'm not sure where right now, but I want us to go to the next level. I just don't want us to move forward living a lie, nor with anything to hide, let's put it all on the table."

Rome's sits soaking everything in, this explains a lot he thought to himself. Andrea could be intimidating to the insecure type. Her wardrobe was exquisite, and she made everything look good. She switched cars like most women changed designer brands, from the Jaguar XJR to the Range Rover Sport she drove tonight. It was obvious someone was major, because he wasn't convinced her job as a realtor was pulling in crazy numbers, or maybe it was, even with that said Andrea remained a mystery.

"Ok, now it's your turn." Andrea said breaking Rome out of his stupor.

"I don't know that's a hard act to follow."
(Andrea laughs)

Rome went on to explain his latest troubles,
everything from Dre being in a coma to his right hand
being in prison and how he could relate to seeing
someone you love being held against their will. What
really had his mind screwed was the inability to get over
the hump. Everytime he took two steps forward, it
seemed like he took three back.

"So that's $80,000 that I didn't have, down the
drain and now I'm right back at square one." Rome told
Andrea with a look of defeat in his face.

"Well at least you're safe, you'll get back, don't
stress yourself about it." Andrea responds nonchalantly.

"Humph. That's all you have to say huh?"

"I mean you, c'mon Rome let's face it, you
wasn't getting money anyway, you was just getting by."

Rome just sits silent, he didn't know if that was
food for thought or if he should feel offended.

Jan. 2005 – Columbus, OH Federal Building

"8.8 pounds of cocaine, four keylos, damn
Chanel you probably never get to see daylight again.
How old are you?" For the past 2 hours the lead federal
agent Spagel has been drilling Chanel, making her fully
aware of the life, she had ahead of her, if she doesn't
cooperate. "Oh your file says 23, what a waste of
potential, if by the grace of God you are freed again,

213

you'll be about 60, 65." Suddenly, the agents whole demeanor changes, and he hops up and shouts, "You think that scumbag would keep his mouth shut for you? Hell no! He'd be in here singing like a baby, this is an open and shut case, Tommy Lee is going to testify!!" He yells as he dabs beads of sweat off his forehead with his handkerchief.

Chanel sits still in the interrogation room with her game face on, worry plagues her mind, but she refuses to let them see her sweat. Truth be told, in the inside she's rattled.

"You still wanna sit there like a mute huh," the agent asks as he paces the floor. He leans into Chanel's face, so close she can feel his breath. "I'm going to walk out this door and give you twenty minutes to think about this. Let your life flash before your eyes, because you think you have a clue, but you have no idea. I'll let you sit in this fucking room for days if I have too, no phone calls, no water, just me and you." Chanel remains silent and flares her nostrils irritated by his tobacco stained breath. "Oh yeah missy, I crack cookies like you all the time," he says before grabbing his coffee and slamming the door shut.

****

So many thoughts races Rome's mind as he tails behind Andrea's Range Rover en route to her home. It's like as the night progressed Andrea pulled more tricks out of her sleeves. All the while he thought Andrea lived downtown in the Woodward Place Condominiums, but she revealed to him that she bought it 2 years back and was currently seeking a buyer. His phone vibrates, and he answers Andrea's call.

214

"We coming up at the next exit."

"Alright," Rome looked up at the sign that read Farmington Hills, which was one of the richest counties in the U.S., home to Eminem, and the late owner of the Detroit Pistons, Bill Davidson. They pull up to a brick home sitting on a slight hill that could pass for a mini mansion. Andrea pulls into her 3 car garage, parks and lead the way as Rome follows. He was in awe as he entered the walk-in basement which was layed out and large enough to be a house in itself.

"Wa La, Welcome to my home." Andrea said smiling with her arms stretched out.

"So you gone give me a tour?" Rome asks eyeing the spiral staircase from the living room.

"Sure follow me."

The kitchen was top shelf, cherry wood cabinets, an island in the center with a marble countertop. The living and dining area was a mixture of flamboyant and modern, which complemented Andrea's style. Rome took heed of the bookshelf and her extensive library that held a variety of titles. Everything from Sister Souljah, Toni Morrison, and Michael Eric Dyson to self-help books on real estate and fitness. Rome had never read a book in his life and for the first time he was intimidated, yet turned on. Most women he dealt with read magazines like Vibe and Sister 2 Sister, Andrea read Black Enterprise, Essence and the Robb Report. Ironically, the tour ended in her bedroom, Rome flops down on the loveseat.

"Out of all the rooms in the house, this the one you decide to take a seat in huh?" Andrea says with a smile.

"I thought this was the last stop."

"Yeah I bet you did," she responds as she removes the top to her Dior suit and her earrings as well. She starts some bathwater and closes the door on her full size bath. "Baby make yourself comfortable, I'll be out in a sec."

Rome kicks off his shoes and takes a look around. He lifts the comforter on her queen size bed with satin sheets underneath accidentally sitting on the remote, activating the surround system. "Love Calls" by Kem comes through the speakers. About twenty five minutes later Andrea appears in the doorway in a silk lavender robe slightly opened exposing her matching lingerie. She walks towards Rome unbeknownst to him because his back is turned and stands behind him with one knee on the bed and began massaging his shoulders.

"Baby that feel so good, Ohhh..... (moans) What you went to school for this or something?"

"Boy be quiet, I'm not that good." Andrea chuckles and playfully punches Rome in his back.

Rome turns around and witnesses true beauty standing before him, clothes did Andrea no justice, her figure was flawless. A look of innocence covers her face as her robe slides to the floor. They share a rough passionate kiss while Rome stands to his feet palming her backside while attempting to lift her up, but Andrea pushes his chest forcing him back on the bed. He removes his shirt as she unfasten his belt, they're naked

216

in no time. The kissing cease as Andrea backs up and unclasps her bra stepping out of her panties one foot at a time. Her nipples stand erect as well as her caramel breasts. Rome pauses momentarily, taking it all in before making his move. He places soft kisses right above her panty line while letting his hands explore her body. Andrea moans softly and her breathing increases, but she stops him.

"Baby wait, (Rome ignores her pleas) baby hold up wait."

"What's wrong?"

"Baby please be gentle ok, it's been awhile."

"Aw baby that's automatic, you ain't said nothing." (Rome resumes his foreplay)

"No baby, Ohh you feel so good...., no baby you don't understand. Rome I'm so tight I can't even use tampons anymore, so please be gentle."

"Baby lay down, you in good hands, trust me." Andrea relaxes on the bed as her juices run down her leg. He slides his tongue inside her juicebox using a melodic rhythm driving Andrea wild.

"Ohhh baby stop...., stop....," she was begging for mercy, damn near climbing the wall. "Ohh Rome I wanna feel you baby, put it in please!!" she yells making sex faces holding on for dear life. Andrea quivers and shakes from the feeling of Rome just inserting the tip, off reflex she pushes his chest with her hands to prevent further penetration, fighting for pleasure. Rome forcibly knocks her hands down and continues to guide his nine

217

inches inside her slippery opening. Andrea's body heat increases as Rome's aggression turns her on.

"Ahhh! Ahh! Ohh! Yes...." Her screams turn into loud cries. Andrea's pussy is so wet and tight that as Rome penetrates the condom gets sucked up and slides off until it is no longer. Rome finds his pace and speeds up his rhythm continuing bareback, the feeling of her creamy releases on his dick driving him crazy. The banging of the headboard muffles her cries, Rome has her legs hoisted up on his shoulders long stroking her as their bodies start to vibrate simultaneously.

"Come with me baby please.....come with me," Andrea cries and tears of pleasure roll down her check. They collapse on each other after a lovemaking session they'd never forget. Andrea hugs him close feeling grateful to find what she'd been missing, optimistic about the future.

****

Ryan Correctional

Don must of paced the 5x9 cell a thousand times in the past two hours. Here he was 4 months until his minimum and it appeared he would be fighting another homicide. "Fuck it, shoot first, ask questions last," Don said under his breath talking to himself, a habit he picked up from being in solitary confinement so much. "Don't stand for nothing then you fall for anything, at least my pride still intact."

"Folsom!! Stand your ass up quit mumbling, you ready to talk yet?" Lieutenant Stokley spoke through the gates, he was new to the prison and couldn't

218

wait to make an example out of someone. "I said get up boy!!"

"I ain't your fucking boy!!" Don yells as he stands eye to eye with Stokley at the gate. He slams his billy club against the cell gates in an arrogant attempt to scare Don, but he doesn't bulge.

"Fuck am I suppose to jump or something?"

"We'll see how long you keep that tough guy act up once it sets in that you're never leaving here. Yeah because that guy you stabbed, it doesn't look like that scumbag going to make it, and as of now we have four witnesses and counting willing to testify and bury your ass!!" Don kept his composure in a military stance holding a mean gaze at Stokley. "Yeah, think about it for a second, ah ha haha….," he walks away in laughter.

****

["The chemistry was crazy from the get-go and neither one of us knew why, we didn't do nothing overnight cause, a love like this takes sometime….,"] Andrea sang along with Mary J as she stood in the kitchen slicing strawberries. "Cause I can't be without you baby!" Rome stood in the doorway chuckling watching Andrea sing backup for Mary. Andrea almost drops the knife becoming startled noticing him.

"Boy you scared the mess out of me!" she says as she turns the music down.

"Something smelling good, my baby can cook and sing huh?"

219

"Yup, I hope you hungry." Andrea set the arrangements on the table looking good as ever, the imprint of her backside could be seen through Rome's t-shirt. Rome taps her behind slightly before sitting.

"Boy don't start nothing now."

"Damn who else eating with us?" Rome stated observing the platter before him. Strawberry pancakes, hashbrowns made from scratch, sausage patties, links and cheese eggs." I might not be able to leave her after this."

"That's fine by me," Andrea says as she seats next to him.

"Ummm, girl what you put in these pancakes.."

"It's a secret." There was a brief silence as the two dug in feeding their faces. "So Rome what's next?"

"I probably slide back to the hospital….," Andrea cut him off.

"No I mean what's next?"

"What you mean?"

"You know, " she said with her head tilted.

"No, I don't know."

"After the game, after you outgrow this hustling stuff."

"Oh so you think hustling is something you just outgrow."

"I know what can happen if you don't."

"Aw man come on not another lecture, you starting already." Rome says as he attempts to stand from the table, Andrea rushes over and stops him.

"No baby I mean what are your goals, your exit plan? Baby understand a person hustling without goals is heading nowhere. You gotta set the bar somewhere or else you get lost and caught in the mix. You look up and regret the fact you didn't buy this land or open this business."

"I know baby, but it's so much shit going on right now, coming at me from all angles. I got plans but first things first I gotta get this money back up." Andrea was now standing between Rome's legs as he starts rubbing his fingers up and down her legs.

"Well maybe I can help you with that."

"Nah, I'm not a charity case and I don't accept donations."

"Oh no, trust me you gone work for it, I can help you if you have goals."

"Yup its right here," Rome slides his hand underneath the tee realizing she's pantyless, he sucks his middle finger before sliding it inside her.

"Ohhh, ohh baby, d-don't start….," Andrea stutters and tenses up before positioning herself on his lap.

Chapter 28

Columbus, OH

Out of habit Chanel sat in the attorney / client visiting room trying to bite her nails, only now they were nibs. The past 2 weeks had been hell for her, her bail was set at a million dollars requested by the D.A. and she was steadily being harassed. One of her associates retained one of the top defense attorneys for her, but she'd be set for trial soon, and she didn't know if she could fit the remaining bill. Rome was missing in action and she'd just been informed that Dre was in a coma.

"30 more thousand, damn you can't go any lower than that, you already got 10 from my friend." Chanel pleaded with her attorney Jon Smitz.

"I'm sorry there's nothing I can do, I already cut $10,000 off my regular fee as a favor to Ramone (Chanel's friend) This is a high profile case, and honestly it's not gonna be easy to beat. I was combing through the discovery last night, and we have a job on our hands. The best I can do is prolong the trial, but I'm only allowed three postponements. But once trial begins I will need to be paid in full...."

"Ok, ok I get it, just give me some time alright." Chanel spoke up before putting her face in her palms.

"The deal is always on the ...." Chanel cut him off beating her fist on the table.

"Look if you say that shit again, you won't have to worry about getting paid because I'm a fire your ass!!! Yall motherfuckers always trying to make yall job easier." The attorney stands to leave.

222

"Alright, I'll see you in a few weeks, and I'll work on that bail reduction."

"You get any answer on that number yet?" Chanel asked inquiring about Rome.

"Nope, matter of fact that number is disconnected."

"I should of known," she said under her breath.

"Yep, well he knows you're here, and for the record Chanel, friends don't treat friends that way." Chanel let his words sink in and begin to think twice about her decision.

****

"Even though he hasn't awakened yet, there's still signs of improvement. His heart rate has picked up tremendously and recovery from the surgery is going well. I'll give you two a minute, if you have any more questions, see me at the front desk." The doctor says while checking his clipboard and Dre's IV before exiting. Rome has a seat.

"Damn playboy you too fly to have these tubes running all through you and shit. Hurry up and come up out of this shit, so we can get these niggas out the way and get back to counting this money." Rome pauses to check his caller ID as his phone vibrates. "It's her again dog, the one I told you about. Man wait until you wake up and meet her, her girls tight too, plus they just your speed. You gone have to boss up though, cause these broads already use to money. She say she got a surprise waiting on me, so I'm a slide before she can change her mind. Don't take too long to wakeup though my guy, or I'm a have to put this work in without you. I can't let

223

you miss that, ain't nothing like the look on a nigga face when he know his time up."

Meanwhile downtown at Fishbone's Restaurant

"Girl are you positive? You sure you trust him like that, plus what Antonio gone think?"

"Antonio don't care as long as he seeing a dollar some type of way."

"Yeah whatever, Andrea I think you playing a dangerous game. You suppose to be getting your coochie wet and having a little fun that's all, don't get caught up." Andrea sat at her reserved table in Fishbone's listening to Tia ramble on and on. A tall male accompanied her in a black suit by Ralph Lauren and 3-quarter Mauri crocodiles. He tapped his watch indicating that time was precious. Andrea held up her finger. "Tia I'm about to hang up, I don't like the way you talking right now."

"Girl you bet not, don't hang up on me."

"Tia he here, I gotta go."

"Alright five minutes," her company said to her before making his way to the bar area to remain seated. Seconds later Rome was walking towards her table, positioned right next to the waterfall.

"Took you long enough," Andrea says as he sits.

"I was at the hospital, what's so urgent, why you all on my head like that?"

224

"Dang, you get straight to the point huh? You hungry, relax order yourself something."

"Naw, I'm cool I really don't have no appetite."

"C'mon Rome, don't be like that."

"Don't be like what? Surprises make me uncomfortable, you rushed me down here, now let's get to the point."

"Ughhh…, I do not like you right now." Andrea says in a joking manner before reaching in her purse and placing a U-Haul key on the table. Rome's body language changes and he tenses up.

"What's that?"

"Your surprise."

"You asking me to move in with you?" Andrea remains silent and laughs softly. Rome sits looking on confused.

"No, but that would be nice." Andrea cut her eyes as the gentlemen who accompanied her earlier gives her a slight nod as he exits.

"Baby the other day, when I met your family and saw you interact with them, I saw a whole nother side of you. In so many words, I saw your goals, your purpose and the responsibilities you accepted proudly. I appreciate you introducing me to your world, and now I want to introduce you to another part of mine. Honestly and loyalty is big to me baby, and I wouldn't ask nothing of you I don't demand from myself. A small U-Haul truck will be parked in front of this address." She slides a folded sheet of paper over to Rome. "Memorize it and destroy it. A nice package will be waiting for you in the hatch inside a furniture set. We'll meet her again next week, same time same table, your ticket is $67,5, I expect you to be ready by then, you alright?"

"Yea I think I'll take that drink now though, Rome says and they both smile. "But naw, I'm relaxed, you know as long as you talking money, I'm cool."

"Can you handle that?"

"Fa sho, what is it like 3 or 4?"

"Five."

Rome calculated the math in his head and realized he was getting them for $13,5 a piece.

"I want you to know this won't affect our relationship or the way I feel about you, so don't start acting funny on me."

"Baby you know me better than that."

"Alright, alright baby, no more surprises, but work with me, you know it's been awhile since I loved someone...," Andrea caught herself covering her mouth as the L word slipped out.

"I love you too."

Rome: "Well it didn't exactly go like that, but I guess it was close enough."

Rio: "Man I can't win for losing with you, the structuring of a story is harder than you think.

Especially when you got someone butting in every chance they get."

Rome: "I understand all that, but don't get mad at me cause I got high standards. But anyway, they say your 2nd connect is always the winner, the one that's gone get you over the top. I ain't gone lie, a nigga was feeling good. I felt like 'KG' (Kevin Garnett) when he was traded to the Celtics, all this time I was content with just making the playoffs, I finally was about to win a ring, I just needed to get on the same page with my team."

Chapter 29

Summer was approaching, and Rome had intentions on making this one, the hottest to date. Everyday felt like a celebration, the bag was in and the numbers was right. At $13,5 he had room to breathe, and the birds weren't pressed. When Andrea dumped the first five on him, instead of dealing with the hassle of breaking them down, he pushed them out the door at $19,5 clearing a quick $30k profit. Make a long story short, he hadn't looked back since, plus he had something to prove, he knew this was just a test and there was more to come. The plug needed to know that he could move the bag fast and that he was worthy.

"$134,996, 134,997, 134,998, 134,999, 135,000." Rome let out a loud sigh after counting out the 135 grand. His fingertips were numb and he suffered a few papercuts.

"Oh come here baby, let me kiss it," Andrea says while reaching for his hand.

"I told you, you didn't have to count it baby, I trust you."

"So, what time you think it's gone land?" he asks speaking on the work.

"I don't know, it might be a hour, or it might be a day or two."

"Well see what you can do because I got people blowing my phone up. I need more than ten this time, I got a 100 grand of my own money…."

"So, that's all we are is business associates now? Lately that's the only time I ever see you Rome, don't let this shit take over you, remember what we talked about, goals."

"I wouldn't talk business all the time, if you wouldn't keep feeding my head with the bullshit, goals Rome, don't get caught up." (Rome mocks Andrea) "Damn are you my woman or my mother."

"That's cause I care about your ass stupid!!" Andrea yells throwing a vase at Rome, he ducks right on time as it misses his head by inches shattering in pieces against the wall. "Now where your ass going?" she shouts as Rome leaves the premises before he does something he regrets.

Ryan Corrections

Don sits patiently awaiting the arrival of his newly hired attorney thanks to Rome. Lately, every letter Don received from Rome, it was more and more promises, things were starting to sound too good to be true. His whole lingo had changed, and he knew he was out there winning. Don felt rejuvenated everytime he read one of Rome's letters that he always ended with, 'sky's the limit' and 'our time has come.'

At the moment Don was probably the happiest dude in solitary confinement. Not only the fulfillment of Rome's success, but he got a letter from his attorney last week saying he had some news that couldn't wait, which was the purpose of this meeting.

"Mr. Folsom, how are you?" Attorney Murray "Cut the Check" Silbeck asked upon entering.

229

"Shit I'll be good once I get from behind these walls, what's the deal?"

Well let's just say after today, you're one step closer. You've been cleared of all charges concerning Charles Mackey (Charlie), the warden received an open confession last week." Don sits there dumbfounded. Did you just here what I said? You don't look like a man who just got a monkey off his back. You got 3 ½ months until your minimum, with your record and the prisons being overcrowded, I'm sure parole will be granted."

"Who was it?" Don interrupted disregarding everything he just said.

"Excuse me?"

"Who was it, who made the confession?"

"Oh, one second," the attorney says shuffling through his paperwork. "Hmmm…an Alfonso Billings, you ever hear of him?" Don nods his head and smiles.

****

Rome finally gives in and answers the phone after dodging Andrea's calls the past couple days. "Yeah."

"You done playing games, now's not the time to be acting your age Rome!" Andrea's voice booms through the phone.

"Whatsup."

"Baby we need to talk like yesterday."

230

"Business or pleasure?"

"A little of both."

"Alright give me a minute, about a hour, I'll be over, did he land yet?" Rome asks speaking on the product.

"Yea, but I need you to come before then, I got something for you, plus I want you to meet somebody."

Those were the six magic words Rome had been waiting to hear since his first trip to the U-Haul. Good things only last for so long and Andrea was allowing her emotions to cloud her judgment. This meeting was inevitable, and both parties would get what they wanted. Andrea could salvage their relationship, and Rome could continue business.

Andrea sat in wait in her teal Porsche Cayenne as Rome pulled up behind her in a platinum Q56 Infiniti truck. He stepped out in the brisk February weather draped in Al-Wissam and Nike ACG boots.

"Whatsup?"

"Get in we got a nice little ride ahead of us." Andrea says as she adjusts her seat. Silence fills the Porsche as the pair ride along I-75 on cruise control. About a hour later, they were pulling into FCI Milan visitor's parking lot. She woke Rome out of his deep nod and he immediately became uncomfortable noticing he was on federal grounds.

"What the fuck! I know you ain't no fucking fed man, I knew your ass was too good to be true....," he says while fidgeting and looking in different directions. Andreas finds it amusing.

"What's so funny?" he says sternly.

"Are you serious,? Relax, I told you I had someone I wanted you to meet." Rome pauses momentarily, realizing that she's speaking of her ex-husband.

"So all this time that shit been coming from him?"

"What difference does it make? Rome he wanted to meet you and I didn't think it was a bad idea." Andrea states lying through her teeth. After being searched and briefed on rules and regulations, Rome trails Andrea into the visiting room. A short light-skinned muscular man sits awaiting, with a silly grin on his face.

Rome: "Man my ego was fucking with me, what the fuck was he smiling for, was the joke on me or something? She probably had me working for him the whole time. Well I was digging his wife's back out, so I guess we was even, but naw who was I fooling. He'd always have the upper hand because sex is sex, but controlling the mind is a whole nother story. I don't know what she was trying to prove, but I was ready to find out."

Rio: "I bet the readers are too, so I wish you let us get to the point and wrap this thing up."

Rome: "Yeah, yeah, yeah, I'm falling back."

****

Big T sits at the bar throwing back shot after shot, of Patron cashing out. The bartender ducks off to the back to make a quick phone call anticipating a payday. "He on his way out, yall better hurry up," she whispers while watching her back.

["What's my name!! Cash out!!! When I'm off in the club, cash out! 50 shots of Patron!!! Cash out!"] Big T lifts his glass in the air while rapping along with the 'Street Lords.' "Toast to my man Charlie, I'm a ball hard for you my nigga!" Starters, a restaurant on Plymouth Rd., where mostly doughboys frequent was near closing. Big T had almost slept with the whole female staff with the exception of Rachel, which only made him want her more. So far he was feeling like tonight might be his night. He grabs hold of her arm as she leaves from behind the bar to wipe a table down.

"Fuck cleaning them tables, have somebody else do that shit, I'll pay them overtime." By this time Big T is behind her kissing on her neck. Rachel reaches behind brushing his dick purposely while fighting him off.

"Boy be easy, I'll be done in a minute, by the time you finish that off I'll be ready," she says before disappearing to the back again pressing redial.

Jamal picks up on the first ring, "My man already in position I'm just trying to find a parking spot, upp, I got one, so be making yall way out in a minute."

"Ok baby, I love you."

"Rachel now ain't the time for all that shit, get your head together."

FCI Milan

"Damn baby you smell good," Antonio says while hugging Andrea letting his hand brush across her backside. Rome stands in the rear feeling a tinge of jealously as they take a seat.

Andrea and Antonio were like the prototype of the hood love story. Antonio was 2 years her senior and grew up in the notorious Brewster projects. The hustle had been embedded in him since day one, all his life he was known to make a way out of no way. Andrea on the other hand, came from a long line of hustlers. She grew up in Grosse Pointe Park, spoiled rotten but down to earth because she knew where she came from. Andrea's uncles were beyond heavy, plugged in with the Mexican Mafia out in Arizona and Cali. They was getting money hustling when it wasn't cool to do it. From the heroin rush of the 60's and 70's to the cocaine era of the early 80's. Andrea's father Dave was killed in the battlefield on the family's road to riches. When she met Antonio in high school and bought him home for the first time, the two fell in love instantly. Antonio took an oath promising Dave that he would be loyal to his daughter and value her life more than his. It was then that Dave opened the door and made him a part of the family, the rest is history.

"Baby you look uncomfortable," states Antonio.

"Wouldn't you be? I'm sitting here with the only two men besides my father that I ever loved in my life."

234

"I see that's why this meeting was necessary cause you can't help wearing your emotions on your sleeve. How much does he know?"

"Nothing he hasn't met anybody, we've been operating the same way you suggested."

"You think he ready to meet Sam?"

"As fast as he's moving it, I think he's more than ready, Sam already notices the improvement and he been inquiring on how we went from 40 to damn near 60 keys a month in no time."

"Alright I still don't understand why you need me, but I'll talk to him."

"Baby you know how the family feel about you, they damn near value your word more than mine. The first thing Sam asked me, when I put the deal on the table was, "How does Antonio feel about this? Not only that, but baby no one will replace you and you'll always have my heart. I'm serious about him and before I move on, your approval means the world to me." Andrea stands hugging Antonio, then motions for Rome to come over and take a seat.

"I'll call you next week and let you know what the lawyer said," Antonio tells Andrea as she leaves the visiting room. She kisses Rome on the cheek before he takes a seat, "I'll be outside baby."

Chapter 30

Big T stood at the exit with his arm around Rachel pissy drunk tapping his pockets in search of his car keys. "T I got them right here," his man/driver Mel said lifting them in the air.

"See that's what I'm talking about, that's what I pay you for. C'mon baby lets go get this show on the road."

Mel and Rachel led the way impatient with Big T's antics, "Damn baby you make that uniform look good, I know it's something special under there."

Jamal recognizes Big T's voice before they come in plain sight, he cocks the hammer back on his ruger before screwing on the silencer. The parking lot is empty despite 3 or 4 cars. "Fuck it," he says as he posts up. He fires 2 shots soon as the doors open hitting Mel in the side of the head. "Ahhhh! Ahhhh!" (screams) Rachel screams as parts of brain matter splatters over her face.

"What the ....." Big T's senses come alive and he draws his 4-5 while gripping Rachel by her neck. "Bloc ah Bloc ah!!" he lets off a few rounds before retreating back inside the restaurant.

Back inside his Corvette, Jamal is elated but unaware he hit the wrong target. He just opened a can of worms and awakened the dead all over again

Meanwhile downtown at River Place Apts.

It seemed Dana just couldn't catch a break, reality bites could be the caption for this picture. She sits in what used to be her living room weeping with her face in her palms, brown boxes and garbage bags align the walls with her things packed. She tried her hardest to avoid the inevitable, but money talks and bullshit walks. The eviction notice said 30 days, not 31, 32 or 45. When Rhino left he took the support of the Hell-Bounders with him, Dana had nowhere to turn or no one to reach out to. She wipes her tears with the back of her hand and reaches for the only answer she had to her worries lately. Yeah, the little white girl, she could always depend on her. "Sniff…, sniff…" She tilted back enjoying the head rush, instantly she thought about one more source she could contact, searching her phone book for the number. After no answer on the first number, she dialed Rome.

"Hello who this?"

"Rome whatsup, this Dana, you heard from Dre, I been trying to reach him, but I can't get through. Rome removed his phone from his ear and then looked at it, as if Dana could see his expression.

"Man Dre been a coma for the past 2 months, where you been?"

"For real!! Are you serious? Well let me know when you see him again, so I can go visit."

"He up at St. John's off Mack Ave., whenever you wanna check for him…" Dana hung up before he could finish feeling no remorse as she searched her brain for another prospect.

Macomb Correctional Facility

Don,

If you reading this hopefully by now you got the news. I
ain't trying to save face or make up for what I did, cause
I know it ain't no coming back from that. Them niggas
could of killed you dog, and I ran off like a little bitch
with my tail tucked between my legs. We born and bred
on the same blocks and we wasn't raised that way. On
the real I ain't been able to look myself in the mirror
since that day. So, when you touch I hope this is your
last memory of me and not that day in the yard. Till we
meet again, hold ya head out there. REAL NIGGAS DO
REAL THINGS.

Much Love,

Speedy

Don stood looking out the cell window reading
the letter from Speedy. In this day and age it was every
man for himself and eventhough Speedy left him for
dead, he still wasn't obligated and didn't have to take the
rap. Don gained a newfound respect for him, cause
honestly he didn't think he had it in him. "30
motherfuckin days, ain't that something." Don
whispered to himself. It had been a long 8 years and he
was ready to turn the streets upside down. Though he
was transferred to Macomb Correctional, his reputation
followed him. On his new block inmates broke they
neck trying to start convo or offer they hand, Don picked
the phone up to call Rome.

"What's the deal playboy?"
238

"Aw man waiting on you to touch, so you can help me count some of this money. I need a nigga who gone appreciate this shit as much as me."

"You already know," Don responds edging him on.

"Hell yeah, I remember us copping work, not even having enough dough left to buy the baggies with until we made our first sale. These niggas ain't never seen the struggle, out there in the freezing cold. Walking out the spot smelling like kerosene, shit slow than a motherfucker, sharing coney dogs, going half on a nickel bag. Now ya boy don't even unwrap them no more..."

"Woah, woah, slow down, watch how you talk on this hot box, you know they listening."

"Man fuck them, I'll buy the state, I'm only worried about the alphabets."

(Don chuckles on the other end) "What you buzzing, you high or something nigga?"

"High off the life that's about it. How many whips you want when you get out my nigga? We might have to get you one for every year you missed." (Rome laughs as he talks) "Feel me?" (You have 60 seconds)

"Hey my time up, I'm a catch you tomorrow, but yeah we might have to do that."

The game had him, Rome's addiction was on full blast. When it came to the hustle, he was sort of like Pookey on New Jack. Rome left FCI Milan with a new ally and a lower ticket, Antonio blessed him and lowered

239

the ticket to $10,000 with the promise that he can handle a heavier load. Antonio respected the game, when they first met he broke the ice informing him that him and Andrea had his blessing and there was no hard feelings. His love for Andrea would never change, but he respected her decision and thought they made a good team. "Don't ever play with her heart, but more importantly don't ever play with our money," were the words he left Rome with. Since then they're relationship had grew, and Rome had even been up to visit again.

The block looked like an auto show exhibit. It was the warmest day of Spring thus far and all the big boys were out from the old to the new generation, fresh from the car wash. Directly or indirectly most of the cocaine flow in Black Bottom and the lower east side went through Rome. His ticket was so low, he cornered the market, and not to mention he was never out. He sat in the driver seat of his Benz CL55 with the door open prepping Kameesha for her trip. Chico was meeting her halfway for his usual ten a week. Jamal sat in the passenger seat playing on his Blackberry.

"Where your girl at, I thought she was riding with you?" Rome asked Kameesha.

"She sitting in the van all nervous cause she saw all yall out here."

"She could of came and said hi." Jamal shouted from the passenger side.

"You got everything you need right? Stop and put that money up before you get on the road, I don't want you riding with all that cash."

"Alright, but Rome you didn't have to pay me no five grand for no hour and a half ride, you gave me enough for 4 or 5 trips last time." Kameesha said before walking off.

"She talk all that shit like she don't want the money, but I bet you, she won't give it back."

"C'mon man, it ain't about the money with her, you act like you don't know what she really want," Jamal responded referring to the crush Kameesha had on Rome for the longest.

"Yeah whatever, let's get back to the point though, Mal how the fuck you miss this nigga and kill the driver? Fuck was you scared or something nigga, shooting with your eyes closed? Now he really gone be on point cause he know we on his head."

Rome: "Never send a boy to do a man's job, they never lied when they said that one. Send this boy on one mission without holding his hand and he can't even get it right. A scared nigga a kill, but a scared nigga will also get you killed or buried under the jail."

Rio: "At the end of the day, it's your fault, you wanna be a boss, you gotta pay the cost."

Rome: "I agree."

Rio: "Alright then, enough said, if you wanna vent, see a shrink, now sit back and let the readers enjoy."

"Baby how you know he don't wanna come home with a low profile." Andrea says over the phone as she tails behind Rome in a '05' Maserati that he bought Don for a coming home present.

The past 6 months had been good to Rome, he cleared $750,000+, got his family a house and they didn't even wanna move. It just sat fully furnished until they were ready. It's no doubt he had M's in his future, they were in arms reach. The bag was consistent and even Andrea had got caught up and eased up off his back about goals and getting out. Instead she was busy trying to mask her jealousy of Rome and Antonio's relationship.

"If that's too much, he can get the CL, it's all good." Rome answered as they pull up outside the Macomb Correctional Facility. Andrea steps out the Maserati and gets in the passenger side of the CL55 Rome is driving. Don stands outside the fence at a loss of words, June 27, 2005, this will be a day he'll never forget.

"Nigga don't just stand there come show your man some love!" Rome shouts bringing Don back to reality. They share a tight embrace. "I miss you boy." Rome whispers in his ear. Don attempts to get in the CL. "Uh huh," Rome stops him and lifts the keychain. "What you think this pretty motherfucker for, I'm riding with you playboy."

"This me?" Don asks his voice filled with excitement.

"You must of thought it was a game or something, hell yeah that's you my nigga, lets ride!"

Rome tosses him the keys and walks to the passenger side.

"Baby I'm a catch you later ok, " Andrea says standing in between the two.

"Alright." Rome barely acknowledges her, not even taking the time to introduce her to Don. Her feelings are crushed, but she understands.

"Let me see your phone, so I can call Dana and let her know I'm out."

"Man fuck Dana."

"Chill dog, don't act like that."

****

The aroma in the hotel room is atrocious. Clothes and half opened luggage is scattered across the floor, and housekeeping was a no-show as sex and cocaine filled the air.

"Uhhhh…, Uhhh…, (moans) Ahhh!!! Ah!!!" Dana releases screams of pleasure as Rhino gives her backshots to remember. "Yes, give it to me daddy, yes, yes!!"

"You like that, don't you," he smacks her ass hard as he penetrates. In the background Dana phone rings for the umpteenth time. Just as Rhino releases, it stops and rings again, he answers angrily. "Hello."

"Speak to Dana." Don has the music thumping in the background on the other end.

"She busy right now." Click….
243

"What?"

Meanwhile Dana sits in the bathroom on the toilet asshole naked. The City Airport Inn on Conner & Gratiot is now where she calls home, unfortunately. The Inn was a hole in the wall hotel, home to mostly prostitutes and small-time dealers. It was Disney Land to those in search of a fix and a quick nut. When Rhino finally decided to answer her call, he was ecstatic to find out this was her new place of residence. Dollar signs came to mind and in his own sick way, he also missed Dana. His plan, use Dana's desperation to his advantage and make her situation profitable. Her self-esteem was at an all-time low, and he'd been working off that, feeding her head with bullshit selling her dreams.

"This gone be easier than I thought," Rhino said as he peeked through the bathroom door. He went unnoticed as Dana was busy holding the foil steady heating the cocaine, prepping to freebase. She sucked the pipe for dear life inhaling the smoke as it rose from the foil. She cursed Rhino when he first introduced the idea of freebasing to her, but at this moment nothing could replace the euphoria she felt.

Don and Rome spent the day tearing down the malls and the boutiques, Rome didn't even give him a chance to spend quality time with his family. Don wasn't a big fan of jewelry but they finished it off with a trip to see Johnny at Zeidmans. In the streets of the 'D,' you ain't did it until you went to see Johnny, a jeweler who was the Jacob of Detroit. Prada sneakers on his feet, the pockets of his Red Monkey jeans had the mumps as Don and Rome led the entourage carrying two Louie knapsacks with $60k in total. They walked in the Sting Gentlemen's Club with plans of making a statement. The group was about 20 deep, most of them Don didn't know with the exception of Ronnie Moe and a few other oldheads from Black Bottom. The rest were younguns from the hood who were whippersnappers, when he left or dudes who were on Rome's line.

"Man we bout to go nuts in this bitch!!" Rome shouts as he aligns the stacks on one of the booths. Don's on cloud nine still trying to catch up, everything moving so fast to him. Half naked and naked women roam the floor, they all look like runway models and video vixens. A red-bone performs on stage doing the splits, making her ass clap in slow motion while licking one of her nipples. A 5'2 chocolate voluptuous woman and a tall yellow petite lady resembling Candace Parker soap up each other in the glass shower. All eyes are on Rome and the crew, they occupy six booths, so many bottles on the table, they have to stand so you can see their faces. Liters of Goose, Ultimate, Moet and some of the players held bottles of Dom. Dancers and female visitors crowd around them anticipating a thunderstorm, making it rain was a way of life for them.

["Patty cake, patty cake baker's man, these other rappers square, I'm so paid!"] Jeezy thumped in the background as money fell from the air like confetti. Don looks around at them like they were crazy and blatantly starts to pick the money up off the ground stuffing it in his pockets. Rome catches him and stops him throwing it back in the air.

(Rome yells over the music) "Nigga that shit ain't nothing we here now, I'm telling you, it's nothing. Rome hugs Don by his neck, he continues to look confused. "Man throw that shit in the air dog. They love us in here, look at them scrambling for that shit."

245

He says while handing Don two more stacks off of the table. The girls clutter around them, the money is falling faster than they can pick it up. Don sips his champagne and falls in line going berserk with the money showering the stage. ["Then I'm gone stack some more, and then what..., stash the rest of the yams in my auntie house."] He raps along with Jeezy smiling.

****

That same night

Tia sits in the passenger side of Ski's 645 in the parking garage at St. Johns hospital. She adjust her uniform after a lunch break quickie. Since Dre been under Tia's care, she asked for more hours, and these rendezvous with Ski has been her only time for sex.

"How Dre doing?"

"He doing better, all the signs of improvements are there, we thought we almost had him yesterday."

"That's whatsup, cause me and JJ miss you," Ski responds while grabbing his crotch.

"Uh huh, you is too much, I gotta go I'm already ten minutes late. I'll call you when I get off." Tia speed walks back to her post, opting to take the stairs, she catches the elevator instead.

"You dropped something," the male doctor says picking up Tia's I.D. badge.

"Oh, thank you so much. Minutes later she finally reaches Dre's room, upon entering she's disappointed to see that his IV hasn't been changed, meaning someone wasn't on their job.

"What I tell them about….," Tia speaks under her breath as she puts on her gloves. She stops and frowns noticing Dre's pillow covers his face. "What the hell…," she whispers before lifting the pillow. "Ahhhhh!! Ahhh!!! (screams) Oh my God!!! Ahh!!!" Tia screams her lungs out while jumping up and down. Dre has a bullet hole in his head the size of a bagel as blood covers his face dripping down his forehead. "Ahh! Help! Help!" Tia screams and runs out the room crying her eyes out.

Chapter 31

"Jamal we've given you 3 weeks and you still haven't produced anything credible. I'm starting to think, you are pulling my leg, I'm running out of patience.

The JANI-KING janitorial service van sat on the secluded block with three federal agents and Jamal sitting in the rear sweating profusely. So busy trying to prove himself to Rome, now taking the hit on Big T was the biggest regret of his life. Not only did he miss his target, but his homework was sloppy, he was unaware that Starters had installed hidden cameras on the outside of the building. To make matters worse, Big T had been under surveillance by the Feds for the past 6 months. So, Jamal fell right into their hands when he committed the murder, which was one crime they refused to overlook for the sake of their investigation. When Jamal first agreed to cooperate, he hadn't planned on living up to it, he just wanted to make bail before Rome found out, but lately they had been everywhere he turned. The feds had him losing sleep and losing weight.

"So, what's its gone be? Remember we doing you a favor, so act like you appreciate it." The agent in the driver seat stated arrogantly.

"Man I told you I got you, this shit take time, I don't wanna raise no eyebrows. We got a big sale coming up soon, about 20 birds, some dudes from Chicago."

"Is this the same big sale that's been coming up for the past 2 weeks. Man c'mon, stop with that bullshit." Now the agent was turned around looking

Jamal directly in the eye. "I mean you only 18, if you wanna spend the rest of your life in prison, then let me know."

Jamal sits quiet for a second before responding, "Man I got you, trust me, it ain't like I'm going anywhere, get with me next week I gotta go meet somebody right quick," he says as he attempts to open the door to leave. The agent in the backseat grabs the door handle blocking his path, then raises his voice.

"Man you think we playing with you, you're not going anywhere!! Jamal we done playing this game with you, time is not on your side. It's time we take control of the investigation, here," the agent retrieves a wire with a listening device attached.

"I'm not wearing that shit!!"

"Humph, like you have a choice, your way is not working, so were going another route. Or we can take you down to the station right now, what you wanna do?"

"Alright, alright I got something for you, about a murder that went down in Southwest about a year and a half ago, a dude named Omar....."

****

Andrea sits on her laptop logged on to EXOTICGETAWAYS.COM setting the particulars she was planning for her and Rome. They were due for a vacation and she was in desperate need of some private time with her man. Andrea felt she needed to get Rome away from Detroit so she could talk some sense into his head and they could start planning their life together. Everything was moving so fast, and they both were guilty of losing sight of the big picture. She made Rome open several accounts with her uncle's connects overseas. Since day one, she made sure he gave her at least $20k a flip to deposit faithfully. He was so caught up in the life, he never paid attention to the balance, which was now at a mil 2 with $300,000 of her savings. Just about what they needed to get their own franchise up and running the 'Hip Hop Café.' She planned on breaking the news to Rome over Pina Coladas at a resort in the Bahamas. Andrea leaves her laptop to pick up the mail from the front door, shuffling through it she notices a letter from Antonio. This is odd, considering they stopped corresponding since she introduced him to Rome.

She opens it anxiously:

Dear Peaches, (smile)

Remember I use to call you that, you hated it at first, but it eventually grew on you. Whenever you heard that name, you knew what mood I was in. (smile) Well, this letter may come as a shock since our writing has been limited to special occasions. (unfortunately) I want you to know my love for you has never changed, (Andrea eyes water and chest becomes heavy as she reads on) I'm still in love with you, like the first day we met at that high school swing out and you took my fitted cap and didn't give it back until the end of the party. (smile) But anyway now for the good news, my lawyer contacted me yesterday and said my conviction was overturned. Come to find out, the lead prosecutor and my trial judge were having an affair on the low. (?) I don't know how that motherfucker found out or got the proof, but all that money I been feeding him paid off. The D.A. got 30 days to fight it, but the (lawyer) said it's doubtful. Don't tell Rome, I wanna deliver the news to him in person, tell him to come see me A.S.A.P. Couldn't wait that long to tell you….Rome pulls up before Andrea can finish the letter, she folds it up for some odd reason, feeling guilty.

The Citgo station on Mt. Elliot and Mack Ave., was bustling with traffic, the four corner radius was full of movers and shakers. It was the first of the month, pimps, fiends, and tricks surrounded the area, hustlers posted in front of the store to make sure nobody cashed their check without giving them they cut. Don had been riding around the hood all day in his Maserati with no destination like a teenager who just got his first car. In Black Bottom, he was the talk of the town, the hustlers wanted to get on, and the hoodrats wanted him alone, if only for one night. Don pulls up to the gas station for the hundredth time.

"Don let me pump that for you." Dave the bum asks. Don passes a twenty and walks towards the store. Dana notices him heading her way and instantly becomes embarrassed. Don already notice her, so it's too late to turn back. She looks a hot mess, her hair is all over the place, in a fuzzy ponytail. Heavy bags under her eyes, and she's wearing that tired ass leather Hell-Bounder vest in the blazing heat.

"Dana! Whatsup, where you been hiding?" Don asks trying to mask his disappointment.

"Hey baby." She embraces Don tightly, he smells a slight stench, flaring his nose. "I heard you was home, I just was trying to put something together, before I reached out."

251

"C'mon now, you know that ain't necessary."

"Yeah I can see that," Dana says nodding towards his car.

"So what you a Hell-Bounder now?"

"Naw that's old news, I only wear this shit when I need it to serve a purpose." Don switched gears.

"So whatsup, what you about to get into, you got a new number or something, what you drinking on?" He reaches for the brown bag she's carrying, but she shys away.

"Oh this ain't nothing, this for somebody else." Dana says embarrassed of the half pint of Mad Dog 20/20 she was holding. "Why don't you give me yours and I get with you later on."

"601-6779"

"Alright tonight for sure."

"Yeah make sure you do that." Don walks back to his whip shaking his head like damn, Dana was looking and smelling foul.

"Don't sweat it young buck, I seen it happen to the best of them," Dave tells Don as he closes his door. He pulls off refusing to believe his eyes.

Chapter 32

FCI Milan

The following week

"Damn man, I'm happy to hear that," Rome stated after Antonio relayed the news of his release to him. In the back of his mind, Rome didn't know how he really felt. Did Andrea know and what were his plans? This would be the true test of their relationship eventhough the past nine months, they bonded like brothers. Rome would never admit it, but in a lot of ways, he looked up to Antonio.

"That's whatsup, now you can come home and help me with the operation."

"Why what's wrong?" Antonio now knew Rome well enough to know when there was a problem and he was hinting at something.

"Shit crazy, Dre just got knocked off in the hospital. I'm ready to kill everything moving, family, friends, anybody that know this nigga! That's another reason why I came up to holla at you. I need you to plug me in with them soldiers you always speaking on, what you call them the Hit Squad?"

"I was wondering when you were gone cash in one of your coupons. But that's why I respect you because after all this time, you never asked me for nothing. You got a lot of pride, but don't let that get in the way of your progress. You remind me of one of my nephews." Antonio relaxes and rubs his chin before continuing. "I remember he ran into a problem awhile back, not too long before I got locked up. He wasn't

253

nothing but like 17, 18 at the time. Good kid, school boy type, grew up in Southfield. All my life, I tried to make it easy for him, I mean this my older sister's son, but he like my own. So one day my sister catch him in the basement loading up a 357, black sweats, black skully on and all that. The little nigga call himself going to put in some work right. (A slight pause and they both laugh) Anyway, she play like she ain't see nothing and call me. I rush over there, "nigga what's going on? He play nonchalant like ain't nothing popping, so I ruff him up tell him, I ain't gone ask you no more." His eyes water and he break down and tell me whatup. So make a long story short, this nigga been hustling behind my back the whole time. Somebody done sold him some bold work and him and his man's going to get at him. I'm fucked up about this like damn, he was doing this shit right under my nose. But I respect the fact that he doing it on his own, and not settled with being spoiled. So I'm not gone let them go by theyself. I tell him ok "let's ride!" We pull up to some apartment building in Southwest, I can't remember exactly, somewhere off Fort St. The guy we looking for car not outside, so they ready to use that as an excuse to back out. "Uh huh," fuck that he might still be in there, I tell them. So they hustling out the building or whatever, I think it had like 4 floors. We use a decoy crackhead to get us up in there…."

"Was it a brown building?" Rome ask noticing the familiarity of the setting.

"Yeah I think so, this was a minute ago, but look we get in there right, ramsack his shit and everything, he ain't in there. But this young cat in there working or whatever, and I'll never forget him, dude had a lot of heart. They run his pockets and smack him upside the

254

head a couple times, then they try to skate. I stop them dead in they tracks. If you gone be in this game, know that you gotta play for keeps, send a message, or you'll be ripe for the taking everytime. I put the two in his head and made them watch. We ain't never find ol boy, but I bet you he never sold nobody else a bold package after that, but the moral of the story is ….,"

Rome interrupts. "Hold up, what year you say this was?"

"Ummmm.." Antonio wrecks his brain. "I fell in 99, so it had to be like 98.'

All Rome was missing was a pistol because the look in his eyes told it all. This whole time, he'd been sleeping with the enemy, Jake was probably turning over in his grave. Fuck your message, is what Rome really wanted to tell Antonio. "I can't believe this shit," Rome says not realizing he's talking out loud.

"What you say?"

"Oh nothing."

"But yeah, 21 days Rome, the D.A. only got 21 days, then I walk up out of here. This a be good because Uncle Sam wanna meet you and I'll be able to introduce yall personally."

"Uncle Sam?"

"Sam the person you need to know, I think you ready to meet him."

"Oh, that Sam yeah, yeah for sure." Antonio might as well been speaking in tongues because Rome wasn't trying to hear it. His mind was on something else right now, putting Antonio's brains on his sleeve.

The ride home was a long one for Rome as he had a lot to think about. His flight with Andrea was set to leave in the morning, but right now a vacation was the farthest thing from his mind. So many questions circled his head, but he came to the same conclusion, Antonio had to die. He pulls up to Chuck's Body Shop on French Rd. hoping to get a piece of mind.

"Boy you must want me to get indicted with you, driving that hot ass car over here." Chuck stated seriously.

"Chill out old school, you always paranoid." Rome says getting out the CL55.

"As long as I think they coming after me, they'll never get me. Once you forget that, and start thinking you untouchable, that's when it all falls down."

Rome nods.

"So what's on your mind young'un?"

Rome spent the next 20 minutes giving Chuck a rundown of the latest events. Chuck was silent as Rome spoke, which was unusual for him.

"Rome what you in it for?" he cuts him off.

"Huh?"

"You heard me, what you in it for, the fame, the money, what?"

"I just wanna make sure my family good, and live comfortably……"

"Bullshit!!! You already accomplished that, so what are you in it for? That's the thing, you can't even answer me. Once you no longer have an answer to that question, it's time to get out. But naw, you ain't gone do that cause she got you sprung, your nose wide open and you don't even see it. The game a bad bitch ain't it?" (Chuck smiles) "Badder than any bitch on the planet."

"So what would you do?"

"First of all I wouldn't of been at no prison visiting no nigga anyway. Only way you catching me on federal grounds is if, I'm in custody. But everything happen for a reason Rome, think about that. Real men live off principles, you can't put no price tag on that, ask yourself what are yours?"

****

Andrea paced the house packing her and Rome's things for their getaway. The last few days she had been trying to console Tia because for some odd reason, she felt like Dre's death was her fault. Andrea cut her short, it was time for her to focus on herself, she spent the remainder of the day getting some much needed me time. Now her mood was cheerful as she danced around the house to the sounds of Jamie Foxx. She checks the time, then dials Rome, "Baby where are you?"

"I'm on my way, I just gotta meet Don on the block right quick, then I'm straight to you."

"Alright, hurry up our flight leave in 3 hours."

257

Rome pulls up to Ms. Patti's (his grandmother) house on Mt. Elliot just as he finished the call, he runs inside.

"Bout time boy." Carrie says reaching her hand out.

"Dang that's the first thing you think about when you see me, ask me how I'm doing first."

"I'm sorry bruh," Carrie hugs him. "Now let's ride because I don't wanna get left."

"Grandma if Don pull up tell him hold tight, I be right back." Rome kisses her and makes his way out the door with Carrie in tow. He shuts the door on his car and sits fumbling with his keys. Rome raises his head and gets the shock of a lifetime. "FBI! FBI!! STAND DOWN NOW!! FREEZE!! FBI!!!" Agents have him surrounded, swarming from everywhere in unmarked Yukon's and Grand Prix's. Rome is boxed in, in a no win situation. Carrie's eyes bulge looking like they're going to pop out of the socket. Don rides pass and keeps going witnessing the worst.

"What the fuck I do!" Rome asks.

"Don't play dumb, you know what we here for, spread them!"

"Carrie, tell moms to call my lawyer!"

Andrea dials Rome for the 20th time, still receiving no answer. Now she's worried, pacing around the house nervously. "Where's he at!" Her mind is on overdrive searching for answers. The phone rings, she answers anxiously.

258

"Speak to Andrea?"

"This is she, who is this?"

"Don." Andrea cuts him off.

"Don where is Rome, we gotta be at the airport in 20 minutes!!! Put him on the phone!"

"Andrea calm down, he wanted me to call you, they got him."

"Who?"

"The Feds picked him up outside of his grandmother's house about a hour ago." Andrea drops the phone and slides down the wall, she weeps uncontrollably. "Hello. Hello! Andrea you there? Andrea …."

****

Windsor, Ontario, Canada

3 days later

"Baby how long you wanna stay down here because my family is bugging me, they can't wait to meet you." Rachel stated to Jamal as the two sat over dinner in Casino Windsor discussing plans to visit her family in Toronto. She was elated that Jamal finally gave in to her pleading to meet her parents. Jamal had his own motives though, which was hiding out from Rome and the Feds. He knew once they picked Rome up, it was only so long before he was exposed. The Feds took their foot off his neck for one second and that's all he needed to skate across the border.

259

"It's an 8 hour trip right?" Rachel nods. "We should get there around noon or something, tell them we might be staying awhile." Rachel grins and scoots closer to him inside the booth.

****

Inside the holding tank, Rome sits on the concrete slab searching his brain for answers. Before his attorney visit, he felt like he knew it all, and seen it all, but he didn't know the half. So busy watching outsiders he neglected to watch those in his own camp. Silbeck informed him that his case could be beat at the preliminary, Jamal was their only witness, and as of now, his source informed him that he was M-I-A. His advice, sit tight, remain optimistic and let him work on bail. The operation was running smooth with Don at the helm, but Rome had bigger fish to fry. Antonio was set to release in about 10 days and he wanted to be waiting on him.

Andrea sat in her car outside the federal building downtown trying to work up the courage to go inside. After Antonio, she vowed to never put herself in this position again, but to no avail. Here she sat, eyes puffy and teary eyed, scared for the man she loved, it was deja-vu. "Girl get it together...." Andrea says under her breath letting out a deep sigh. Five minutes and a flight of stairs later she found herself behind the glass with the receiver in her hand. Rome look like he hadn't slept in the 4 days he'd been there.

"Whatsup? What's wrong you been crying?"

"You can tell."

260

"Yeah. Baby I'll be out of here in a minute, they just trying to throw anything against the wall to see if it stick. They don't have nothing, and I ain't did nothing." As he talks, Andrea nods slowly, her eyes off in space as if she's somewhere else. "My preliminary hearing on the 8th, I should be out by then, don't stress ...."

Andrea intervenes. "Baby I talked to the lawyer, Rome I can't do this."

"What you say?"

"I said I can't do this," she emphasizes with her hands. "I'm not prepared mentally or physically to deal with this, my heart can't take it, I just don't know what to do ...." (she begins to sob)

Rome sits enraged, his eyes telling it all, "I guess not since your boy on his way home, I should of expected this ......"

"Is that what you think this is about?"

"Man beat your feet!!!"

"Excuse me?"

"You heard what I said, damn give a nigga a chance to ride upstate first before you leave him in the cold. I read this book before, I already know the ending." He slams the phone down and storms off. The tough role is an act, deep down he's hurt and feels betrayed.

****

"Yall still ain't heard from Mal huh?"

"Nope that nigga number changed, and he ain't even been by here to pickup his money, that ain't like him neither." T-Dot and Lonnie stood on Ludden St. as Don questioned them. Jamal was gone be easy to find once it was out, a tag was on his head.

"You know what Don, check with his girl that work at Starters, she might of seen him."

"What girl that works at Starter's?"

"Her name begin with a R or something, Rachel I think it is, light skinned thick ….," Don was distracted by the arguing from behind the gas station.

"Where my change at Sunshine, don't play with me. A half pint of Seagram's only $6 and two loseys …."

"Girl please, you owe me that from the last time I looked out, fuck you, I need mine!" Sunshine said before trying to walk off. Dana snatches her by the collar, "Bitch who the fuck you think you playing with!"

Don shakes his head watching the whole scene play out, Dana is wearing the same exact clothes he saw her in last week, and it looks like she hasn't took it off since then. She even look ten lbs. lighter since their last encounter.

"Dana!!" Don yells for her attention, she's so busy scuffling she fails to hear him. "Fuck it." Don gets in his whip and pulls off. Unbeknownst to him, a black Navigator follows him two cars back.

262

Inside the truck, "Man we should of spilled him right there, them other two niggas wasn't strapped."

"Naw that's too mediocre, we gone make these niggas flee the country for what I got planned for this one." Big T states from the passenger side with a devilish grin.

****

August 5th '05'

"Just the man I wanted to see, tell me something good." Rome rubs his palms together as his attorney sits.

"Well ...., no word on my motion for bail yet, but the preliminary is still set for this Friday."

"Ok so that's only 3 more days...."

"Hold on, let me finish. My source says they still have no word on Jamal's whereabouts, so we don't have to worry about him, eventhough his statement is what's holding you, without him testifying, it really won't hold any weight. Rome I could care less if you're innocent or guilty, I'm gonna get you out of this, but I need you to be completely honest with me, that's the only way I can help you. Is there anybody else that can tie you to this or anything that can hurt us? We can't afford any surprises."

"No, I already told you that."

Silbeck sighs and takes a deep breath, while pulling some paperwork out of his briefcase. "Well according to this, you're a liar and we go back too far for

263

me to give you that title. This was sent to my office today through a fax from the Prosecutor's office, they have a new witness."

"Who?"

"Umm, a Renee, Renee Moore, she plans to testify at the preliminary, from their perspective she'll be all they need. All the energy looked like it had been sucked out of Rome's body. His facial expression and body language alone even had Silbeck worried. "So do you wanna answer my question again, we only have 3 days, do we need a continuance?"

The following day

Don sat opposite the glass trying to make sense of everything Rome just dumped on him. Antonio killed Jake over some bold work Omar sold his nephew, and he would be home in a few days. Jake's mother Renee was planning to testify against Rome, shit was crazy how did it come to this? Now the shoe was on the other foot, it was up to Don to hold down the fort.

"Yeah she gotta go dog, I mean it ain't no way around it, my life or hers. She know just enough to bury me, you know it don't take much for them juries." Don just sits nodding his head searching Rome's eyes for any signs of guilt for what he's asking him to do. "If you can't handle it, let me know, and I'll see about getting somebody else on it."

"Naw I got it, that's how we got into this in the first place, everybody not who they say they are. We can't take no chances." Don looks Rome in the eye.

"True."

264

"It'll be done by Friday," he rises to leave, Rome speaks up.

"Hey Don, I owe you my life dog. Trust me it's just as hard for me, as it is for you."

"I know, you ain't gotta tell me that."

Friday Morning

Renee stands in the mirror buttoning her blouse, she fastens the pen with the N/A emblem on the left hand side. She smiles, here she was starting over in the house she was raised in, along with her deceased son Jake. So many memories live on in their home on Concord St., some even brought tears to her eyes, but today was different. Today was special, yes, August 8th, she celebrates 6 months clean. Her eyes water from joy as she looks at her reflection. The road to sobriety was a tough one, which came with tough decisions, one was cooperating with the authorities against Rome. She was done with that life and felt it necessary to clear her conscious, till this day she felt responsible for Omar's death. Those demons just kept coming back to haunt her. "Twenty minutes, let me call and see what's taking her so long." Renee whispers while checking her watch, she picks up the phone to call her sponsor.

"You's a sick motherfucker, you know that?"

"Yeah I heard that before, but you ain't seen sick yet, wait till you see what I got planned for this nigga...." Big T bragged to his man Rell as he maneuvered through traffic behind Don. Don's routine was simple, even as his status grew, he'd yet to break his habit of circling the hood. Hang around Black Bottom long enough and Don would pop up sooner or later.

265

This was Big T's plan, and thus far it had proved successful. This was the first time since they began laying on him that he was dolo, which is what they needed for their plan to work. Box him in, snatch him up, and on to the torture chamber......

Don drives like he never wants to get to his destination, he battles with his conscious until it is no longer, the outside world doesn't exist right now. Renee isn't his friend's mother, she's a target, an obstacle in the way of Rome's freedom. Taking Rome's freedom would be like taking food off his plate, even worse, it would be taking a part of him. This is Don's rational as he parks in front of Renee's house. He takes a long tote of his Newport, cocks the hammer on his Smith-N-Wesson. He steps out the car unaware of the Navigator parking two houses down.

Renee sits in her room reading Psalms, her favorite chapter in the Bible. Renee takes notes prepping for her speech she's set to give at the N/A fundraiser in celebration of her 6 months clean. Two soft knocks echo from the door, "Bout time." Renee rushes to the door anticipating her sponsor.

"Dog, what the fuck you waiting on?" Rell questions Big T.

"You don't see that old lady sitting across the street on the porch stupid. As soon as he comes out we on his ass, it look like she going in the house now. I'm done with the games, if someone with him they going too."

"Do I know you?" Renee asks upon opening the door.

"It's me ma, you don't remember?"

"Ma?" Renee mocks him in disbelief.

'It's me Ma, Don, Jake's friend."

Oohh….my god, Ohhh…." (Renee hand covers her mouth) "Ohh I'm sorry, I didn't even notice you, come on in."

Rome: "I walked in the courtroom with my defense team feeling untouchable. Fitted Armani suit down to my square-toe Mauri big blocks. All black everything, I was trying to make a statement. This might as well been a funeral because as far as I was concerned this case was dead. The first face I seen was Andrea's, fuck was she doing here. Naw, don't get back on the bandwagon now, I don't want you support, I don't want nothing to do with you. Antonio will be home Monday, better rush back and get to him before I do because you might as well stick a fork in him, he's done, feed him to the fishes. Look at the D.A., his face red as fuck, I can tell he's nervous. Why wouldn't he be, looks like everyone a no-show. Yeah I'm walking out this motherfucker like George Jefferson, better yet, John Gotti….."

Bailiff states: "All rise for the Honorable Judge Winthrop, THE UNITED STATES vs. JEROME WILSON…."

Simultaneously, Silbeck's paralegal taps him from behind the defense table, signaling an emergency phone call. "What." Silbeck turns around irritated.

"You have a call, you must take."

267

"Excuse me, your honor. Hello, ok, yes were in court now, ok." After hanging up Silbeck gestures for Rome whispering in his ear, "Rome, I've got some bad news……."

TO BE CONTINUED…………………..

Coming of Age II

"The Other Side of the Fence"

Available Now

Order at prpublications.org or by mail at:

PR Publications LLC

P.O. Box 32985

Detroit, MI 48232

PR Publications LLC
P.O. Box 32985
Detroit, MI 48232
pr_publications@hotmail.com

visit www.prpublications.org to order online with credit or debit card

Order Form

Please Print Clearly

First Name: _____

Last Name:_____

Inmate ID (if applicable):_____

Mailing Address:_____

City: _____ State: _____ Zip: _____

Please fill out for referral program only:

Referred by (if applicable):_____

Inmate ID (if applicable):_____

Mailing Address:_____

City:_____ State: _____ Zip: _____

Titles	Pricing Information	Shipping & Handling
Coming of Age	$15.00 x _____ (Quantity)	$4.95 x _____ (Quantity)
Coming of Age II "The Other Side of the Fence"	$15.00 x _____ (Quantity)	$4.95 x _____ (Quantity)
Total		
Grand Total		

Please remember that no personal checks will be accepted and please make all money orders out to PR Publications LLC. Also, free shipping and handling for all inmate orders. Coming of Age is also available for ebooks at Amazon.com.

Author Bio

Jeremy Mulligan a.k.a. Remy was born and raised in Detroit, Michigan. Stemming from a family who instilled the importance of education in him at an early age; as a youth he was always an avid reader and wise beyond his years. But like so many other black adolescents before, Remy's short-term thinking deterred him from the classroom to the streets. After numerous brushed with the law, at the age of 23, the pitfalls of the drug game landed him in prison serving a lengthy sentence. Now forced to face his newfound reality, rather than sulk in regret, Remy is determined to turn a negative into a positive through his writing. They say one must go through darkness in order to see the light. This life-altering experience has given Remy a new outlook on life and awakened a gift in him, he didn't know existed. A raw fresh voice to 'Urban Fiction', Remy not only aims to entertain, but hopes his stories can serve as a cautionary tale as well.

For more on the author visit him at:

Facebook.com/Jeremy Mulligan

www.remybooks.com

www.prpublications.org

For bulk ordering information or to get on the mailing list for book updates, please contact Mr. Paul Tate at (313) 932-0710 or by email at pr_publications@hotmail.com. Also, visit our website to order with credit or debit card; and for other information concerning PR Publications LLC. No personal checks will be accepted and make all money orders payable to PR Publications, P.O. Box 32985, Detroit, MI 48232. Institutional checks will be accepted as well. The price of the book is $15.00 and shipping and handling is $3.95. Free shipping and handling for all inmate orders.

www.ingramcontent.com/pod-product-compliance
Lightning Source LLC
Chambersburg PA
CBHW070329260626
47160CB00003B/988